# MONKEY GIRL

# MONKEY GIRL

SWINGIN' TALES
BY

# BETH LISICK

MANIC D PRESS
SAN FRANCISCO

Grateful acknowledgments is made to the following publications and recordings in which some of these writings first appeared in slightly different forms: *Revival: Spoken Word from Lollapalooza 94, Plazm, Clockwatch Review, Meow: Spoken Word from the Black Cat,* and *Market Street: Live from the Cafe Du Nord.*

ISBN 0-916397-49-1

Library of Congress Cataloging-in-Publication Data

Lisick, Beth, 1968-
    Monkey girl : swingin' tales / by Beth Lisick.
        p.    cm.
    1. City and town life—United States—Literary collections.
2. Popular culture—United States—Literary collections.    I. Title.
PS3562.I77M66    1997
818'.5409—dc21                                                    97-4728
                                                                      CIP

5  4  3  2

Distributed to the trade by Publishers Group West

# CONTENTS

9    Monkey Girl

12    Flat Rate Rental

14    The Bus Ride of Diminishing Returns

17    Pantoumstone For A Dying Breed

19    Man Comes Up To Me In A Bar No. 6

21    Genki

23    Man Comes Up To Me In A Bar No. 3

25    Messed-Up Triptych

27    Man Comes Up To Me In A Bar No. 4

28    Valentine's Day, San Jose Style

33    The Answer Is Plastic

38    Pear

41    People Pleaser

44    Christmas In TeeVee Land

46    Weekend Warrior

49    The Happiest Place

55    Reaching For Pork

57    Things You Put In A Jar

59    Blankathon

61    Empress of Sighs

64    Long Weekend

66    Crappy Brown Carpeting

69    So Little Sleep So Far

74    Babe and the Bathwater

79    Elegy For A Greedy, Slothful Orthodontist

82    Stuff To Do In Saratoga When You're Bored

85    Devil's Vacation

88    Fix

91    Hairdo

93    Santa Cruz

96    Skinny

98    Sneaky Tiki

101    Nice Pants

104    Unsafe

106    U.P.D.I.

109    Worldwide Animal

112    Worry Doll

114    Nice Is Easy

116    The Call of The Mall

120    Big Shop

MY FIRST BOYFRIEND
SKIDDED HIS BMX BIKE
TO A HALT AND WE DECIDED TO KISS
ON THE COUNT OF THREE.
IT ALL STARTED OUT EASY ENOUGH . . .

# MONKEY GIRL

Oh, Monkey Girl. Oh yeah, Monkey Girl. Gung Hay Fat Choy! I was born in the year of the monkey.

I was walking around the Chinese New Year parade. There I am drinking a warm beer, I had my paycheck in my sock, and this old lady I'm standing next to asks me what year I was born.

"1968," I tell her. "The year of the monkey." That much I'm sure of.

"Oh. Monkey is naughty!" she tells me and clucks her tongue. "Monkey is sneaky. You are naughty monkey, I know."

Well, oh yeah, Monkey Girl. Gung Hay Fat Choy, Monkey Girl!

"I know all about you."

Then one of those guys, the kind working for the environmentally progressive energy corporations in between getting his master's and his bachelor's, approaches me, his gigantic hand extended. "Hi! I'm Steve! I'm a rat."

"Rat is clever," the old lady says. "Rat work hard. Rat make good mate."

"So, why don't we blow this teriyaki stand and get a drink," he says.

I tell him teriyaki is Japanese. Mr. Stanford Rat Boy is not so smart after all. "Yeah. I'll let you buy me a drink."

So I go along with this for a couple of ...months. And I can't even think of my own excuses why at this point. I just keep thinking, monkey is naughty. But he's a rat, and I have to keep reminding myself of that.

I have two recurring nightmares: one about my dad's '77 Pinto and another about rats. I'm naked in my bed and there are big lumps moving underneath my skin. They're rats that have burrowed there except there are no entry or exit wounds. They're just crawling between muscle and skin up my thighs, up my stomach and then busting out where my collarbone breaks. Their hideous yellow-tooth faces look a lot like mine.

The last rat I saw before this guy was in an East Village garbage can snorfling through a bag of used pampers. The rat before that crawled up my pajama leg as I slept in a smelly, drafty studio in Santa Cruz. And then there was Pippin, the only pet that was ever all mine. She choked to death in my fourth grade bedroom on a tennis ped I gave her to sleep in while I was away at my family reunion in the Ozarks.

Gung hey you, you fat choy! You were born in the year of the rat?

Now sometimes I read my horoscope and if I don't like it I can just pretend I'm the self-involved Cancer, the brooding Scorpio, instead of the happy-go-lucky Sagittarius. However, for some reason, I deeply believe in this rat thing. This Chinese lunar calendar business. It must be all that advertising about the mystique of the Orient. Ancient Chinese secret, huh?

Just give me a horse. 1954. 1966. I'll gladly swat the flies from his butt.

Or a snake. 1965. I have no problem sucking poison.

Rooster. '69. I've been known to enjoy a cock.

Dragons. Tigers. Oxen. Cool!

Dogs. Pigs. Rabbits. Sheep. Cute. Kind of '80s country kitchen wallpaper material, but cute enough.

This monkey girl just wants to go to the monkey bars, hanging upside down while all the blood pools inside my head and I think I'm somewhere else. Somewhere far away from Pintos and tennis peds, family reunions, the Ozarks and this dirty, clever, hardworking rat with the six figure income who only wants me because I'm naughty.

## FLAT RATE RENTAL

You reached inside the hood and
disconnected the odometer of the rental car

In those 14 seconds, it only took you 14,
someone started flickering newsreels on the gas pumps
showing me footage of all the other
tricks you knew

I took the first letter of every sentence you spoke that day
and made up acronyms to get at the true meaning
which was just not fair, I'm sure

Unruly perverts were in the house
    overcoming lapses in virtually every sensibility,
became
UP WITH OLIVES

Please. It looks extremely sexy,
became
PILES

Carver is rough, consistent, unaffected. So cash in.
    Reevaluate Carver using semiotics,
became
CIRCUS CIRCUS

It went on like this until I passed out

I woke up relieved, careening toward the ocean
traveling at zero and having covered
no detectable ground

## The Bus Ride of Diminishing Returns

I'm breaking hearts all over town tonight. Taking the bus to do it cause I don't have a car. Riding through the Presidio at midnight after making all the necessary stops to start to get myself out of situations I once wanted in on. It's a good thing all three people live along the 22 Fillmore route this time, so I can just get a Late Night pass and keep moving.

Two weeks ago, maybe even a month, I was so good. Sucking down bottles of red wine, stocking up on massage oil and candles, always perfectly tweezed, washed, and shaven. Wearing my best underwear. Just in case.

I read theater reviews. Maybe we could get cheap tickets to a matinee of *Picasso at the Lapin Agile*. I would cry in languid French films and laugh til I cried in American romantic comedies. Meg Ryan, Tom Hanks, how do you move the collective we?

On the bus tonight, it's me - dried sweat, gin breath, nice shoes me - and six mental patients, all silent except one who keeps leaning over the driver's shoulder announcing, "We're coming through! We're coming through now! We're coming through it all right!" and a group of Latino high schoolers.

"Why you always have to be tagging, ese?" a heavily-powdered girl with lips like a gash says.

"It's in my blood," the boy says. "My father wrote. His father wrote. His father before him wrote. It's in my blood."

I look down at my hands, my fingers are scarred. I really hate it when they start to cry, but it's hard to care about it when you just don't care that much about it. Next stop, me. Time to break some hearts.

"We're coming through!"

The girl starts in, "You better call me, ese."

"Yeah, I'll call you."

"You don't even have my number."

"I'll get it from whatsername. I've got her number."

"Yeah. I bet you got her number."

At first I love charming them, their friends, housemates, assorted relatives, and co-workers. They always enjoy my three good stories. But as soon as it turns into,

"What do you want to do?"

"I don't care. What do you want to do?"

"We could rent that movie."

"I've seen it before, but it's a really good movie."

"No, let's get something new."

" No, it's a really good movie. Let's just get that one."

That's when I pay my fare and start riding, making all the necessary stops.

Lights out, rumbling over hills with a silent driver. Drive her? I don't even know her.

We come around a turn and I can see the city now. I exhale.

You better call me.

I can't help it. It's in my blood.

We're coming through. We're coming through now. We're coming through it all right.

## PANTOUMSTONE FOR A DYING BREED

Until you change your mind
I'll watch you chew the olive from the toothpick
When I told you I finally got my teeth cleaned
I didn't really expect you to reply

I'll watch you chew the olive from the toothpick
as you continue talking about your wife
I didn't really expect you to reply
Nothing lies still long

As you continue talking about your wife
on the side of the interstate
nothing lies still long
and nothing makes you happier

On the side of the interstate
I told you I finally got my teeth cleaned
and nothing makes you happier
until you change your mind

## MAN COMES UP TO ME IN A BAR
## NO. 6

He told me I was a serial seducer, but he understood because he was too. He told me there were only ten people worth knowing in this world, he called them the Sacred 10. They were about to take off to the desert to form their own biosphere, one guy flaked, would I like to come along?

He said they'd been planning this for months, hashing it out in motor lodge swimming pools, eating tater tots, drinking whiskey out of dixie cups. They had discovered Boston's first album.

As if praising the white trash for just breathing would lead to salvation, now that everyday type slacking and brushes with people who have had brushes with fame have become too heavily documented to co-opt into the post-collegiate lifestyle.

"But back to you. I know a lot about you," he says.

The girl on the next barstool issues a warning. "Dude, being a stalker is so mid-eighties."

"Back to you," he continues.

"No, back to you, motherfucker," I want to yell as if I were Miss Liz Taylor in a muumuu and feathered mules at home on a week-long bender.

He starts in. "Serial seducer. Me and you. You and me. Ripped from a lactating tit, we drool our celestial milk on cheekbones and used cocktail napkins wherever we go. Swerving into oncoming lies on feet greasy with Mazola. The crown of our glory made by Mattel, reduced to half price, buried in dirt with pet hamsters and rotting stone fruit. Bursting through doors as if lush piano chords sang with inexorable timbre. Do you know? I know that you know, serial seducer."

It is last call. I check my pocket, swear I lost a twenty somewhere and start counting my drinks backwards, but it all checks out.

Slowly, the lights come up. His lips twist grotesquely. He calls out like a Spanish textbook rooster, "Quiriquiriquiri!" and then gives me the thumbs up as I recline without hesitation onto anything with legs.

# GENKI

He said let's smoke a square
He said let's drink 40s and watch Sumo at a car dealership
He said I can't believe you left all of my paintings
    in the trunk of a Tokyo taxi
He said tell them to give us matching kimonos
He said let's do Love Potion #9 at the VFW bar
He said let's play the story game again
He said let's buy some pantyhose from the vending machine
He said let's go to the Japanese equivalent of Disneyland
He said let's blow all our money on Indian food
He said let me tell you about Mothra
He said let's close the curtains and cave out
He said the trains have stopped running, oh well
He said put the tattoo on my earlobe

He said, I will tell you this, you cannot tell anyone
and I went home and said I really enjoyed Japan
Great food. Good weather. Nice people.

## MAN COMES UP TO ME IN A BAR NO. 3

The lawyer sat down next to me and slid me his card.

"You never know when you're going to need a good lawyer," he said. In the middle of this nightspot, this Spot Most Likely To Get You Feeling Like You're An Extra In One Of The Classic Prince Videos, he comes off semi-attractive in that *Tiger Beat*, brush cut, crocodile loafer sort of way. That two years out of school, pick up the shirts at the cleaners, got my own flat on Russian Hill way. That I'm really into Charlie Hunter, that supper club is so overrated, this bathrobe is from my trip to Milan way. So he was not attractive at all.

But this well-scrubbed cartoon was exactly what I needed to cheer me up. I nodded my way through his neo-conservative Rush Limbaugh For President diatribe, appearing alternately engaged and enlightened. A trick that never fails to bring me amazing material with little or no effort. Also, I have learned from my friend Jose that in situations where polite conversation is bound to fail, it's best to try a different tactic. Maybe it was the gin, but when he confided that his practice was defending corporations against sexual harassment suits because that was where the real money was and ninety percent of the cases are outright lies from money-grubbing divorcees anyway, I started to lose my composure.

Right on schedule, his friend arrives. "Dude! We've got to get to that Rock Against Rape show at the Paradise! Jim's got us on the list! He's gonna to introduce us to that babe lead singer from... what the fuck is that band's name? You know, the one with that babe lead singer."

He throws a large bill at me, which more than paid for the drinks, but didn't quite begin to cover the messes he would leave in his wake. Crossing the floor with identical swaggers they'd probably picked up during Rush Week ten years earlier, they head toward the door - I'm sure on their way to molest innocent women and then deny it, so I yell after them, "See you in hell!"

All the coutured and coiffed patrons glance my way, and the bartender calls over, "Whatever, bitch."

I am grabbing my coat, resolving not to wake up tomorrow morning with the perfect comeback. As I'm sliding in and out of geeky plastic-clad scenesters on my way to the door, I grind through the sedentary deposits in my brain and come up with, what seemed at the time, a winner. I conjure up my best Meredith Baxter Birney CBS *Monday Night at the Movies* expression of sheer terror and scream, "Soylent Green is people!"

You know, sometimes you want to go to a place where no one knows your name.

# MESSED-UP TRIPTYCH

I hear the last strains of your theme song zipping out from the gold fillings in the mouth of the guy standing next to me.

My head snaps back involuntarily and as I'm slowly returning it to its normal position I decide to hum a few bars to show we're simpatico. The guy gets nervous, white-knuckles his dirty Hello Kitty tote bag, clenches his teeth so I can't hear as well. What comes out now sounds like crickets playing a fully orchestrated Morricone piece on Chinese mouth organ. Not bad.

We step on the train.

I don't have a newspaper or bestselling novel.

I read the graffiti on the wall of the house that says SPEAK ENGLISH OR DIE.

I read the writing on the kid's backpack that says R.I.P. TUPAC WE LOVE YOU.

I read the vanity plate that says 1HOTMAMA, and then crane my neck to see if the driver is truly one hot mama or an impersonator.

There is a problem.

The train is not moving.

I read the billboard that says IT'S THE CHEESE.

I read its companion piece GOT MILK?

We make a messed-up triptych, the lactose billboards and me. You glance up and I swear you mouth the words, "Dairy fucks you up."

Your stop is near the Guitar Center where you work. I want to ask you if it's true about the daily morning sales meetings. When a customer says, "How much are these strings?" are you really supposed to say:

"How much are they worth to you?"

"How much have you got?"

"What do you want to pay today?"

"What did they charge you at the other place?"

You look like the type to just say, "That'll be $7.99," but perhaps I am projecting.

What if you got married to a lady who worked at The Gap. After you two finished any kind of transaction, she would lick her lips and smile coyly, "Need any socks today?" You would adjust your belt buckle and answer, "Sure. Need any picks today?" You would live happy as clams. The end.

At the next stop, I climb out onto the dirty street and look for clues. I am sent on a scavenger hunt past churches and dog carcasses, into an empty Thai restaurant, over hills, through a picket line and onto the lawn of the mayor which is covered with yellow Post-It notes. I have seen so many Post-It notes in the past ten years that I instinctively ignore them now and keep going. It feels like I'm getting warmer.

# MAN COMES UP TO ME IN A BAR
## NO. 4

I have a witness for this one.

I'm hanging out by the jukebox at a dive in Long Beach. The overwhelming stench in the air is the unmistakable combo of one part puke to five parts cheap floral air freshener. The guy in the Houston Oilers t-shirt clears his throat, and with nary an introduction, leans over my way and takes an extremely audible sniff. He smiles and says in a voice that can only be compared to Jeff Spiccoli in *Fast Times At Ridgemont High*, "Is that you I smell?"

# VALENTINE'S DAY, SAN JOSE STYLE

It's the middle of the afternoon on St. Valentine's Day. I step out of the shower, wrap a fluffy white towel around my head, slip on the kimono I picked up at a street fair in Japan last year and make my way into the bedroom. I'm acting like I stepped out of a cheesy douche commercial, though I can't get a handle on why. Falling back onto the bed, I am still clutching my bottle of melon/berry/aloe/peppermint clarifying enriching enhancer. I don't know quite what to do with it, but I'm certain now is the time to use it.

It's been sitting in the cabinet ever since I won it at that baby shower a few months ago. I had never been to one before. This is probably old hat for all the baby shower veterans out there, but... they have you play games and shit. There was one where you try to come up with as many possible names for the unborn child out of the letters that comprise the parents' names. Example: Tom and Mary. You could make Ray, Tory, Amy, Mat, Myra, Ty, Ry, Ram, Yma, Tor, Oma, Ramy, Mory, Tammy, Tommy, Marty, Mart, Morty, Mort and Mao. Now you can see how I won.

So I'm there in the bedroom when I spy the standard five-pound box of See's Candies that my mom has given me every year since Carter was president. I am hungry. It's been a long day. I opt for chocolate. I am a bad *Cathy* cartoon and I realize this. I reach over, with a half-eaten caramel in my mouth, and grab the new underwear I bought at Victoria's Secret - three for $10 cotton briefs. Racy! Under normal circumstances, I would never go to Victoria's Secret. In a mall. On Valentine's Day. In San Jose, of all places. Suffice it to say, I was not feeling myself. Visions of the crowded shopping center come rushing back and completely ruin what might have been the first textbook *Cosmo* moment I'd ever had.

"Okay, listen up!" the store manager said in her best head cheerleader rally cry. I secretly wonder what kind of underwear she has on.

"We've sold out of the Valentine's Panty Pouches. I just got a call and a man will be coming in for the last three pairs. Two mediums and one small and that's it. We've completely sold all of the Panty Pouches. Good job!"

The staff begins a brief staccato clap as I glance around hoping to sneak a peek at a Panty Pouch.

Back at home, I hold the underwear up to my face and grab at the tag with my teeth. I'm just spitting out the plastic thing when I hear it.

"Oh. Oh god! Yeah!"

My neighbor is fucking the new girl from downstairs. I had seen them walking in together when I came home.

I get up, go to the kitchen, put some water on for tea, grab a glass from the cabinet, and put it to the wall like I was taught in science class.

I sit on the floor against the wall in the last remaining patch of sunlight and listen to Larry, who always wears Green Bay Packers sweatpants and mildew thongs, and Gina, who parks in my space and bumps into furniture at 4 a.m., laughing on speed.

"Whoa! You're really flexible," he says.

"I usually do it with rockers or stoners," says Gina. "But you're more the football player type. Look at that."

"What?"

"Give me another hit of that."

"How old are you again?"

"I've never done it like that before." Yeah, right.

For a moment, I think of trotting over in my open kimono and offering them a maple soft center with chocolate colored saliva dripping out of the corner of my mouth like the overindulgent, orally fixated vampire that I know, at heart, I am. Or splaying spread-eagle on the floor, slipping a finger or two inside myself and climaxing at the exact same moment as Larry and Gina.

Instead I just crane my neck. Ear pressed to the glass, glass pressed to the wall, Larry pressed to Gina, Gina pressed to the mattress, until they have drifted into sleep. The sun goes down, I have a bad stomachache and my hair has dried in knots and clumps.

THE DAY YOU ARE TEMPTED TO CLIP OUT

A COMIC STRIP AND POST IT ON A BULLETIN

BOARD IS THE DAY YOU NEED

TO QUIT YOUR JOB.

# The Answer Is Plastic

You'd think I could have had a normal teenager job instead of the one I ended up with. Most the kids in my high school who worked did so at one of three places: Marjolaine, the French bakery downtown; Bears In The Wood, a store specializing in expensive teddy bears at the height of the teddy bear craze that followed on the heels of Cabbage Patch Kid mania; and the Argonaut Dry Cleaners. I have no idea what the dry-cleaning connection was, but half of the Spirit Squad worked at the counter after school and on weekends. Ours was not a community where teenagers did the fast food route. So me and my pal Nicole decided to apply at McDonald's. We were only fifteen at the time, but we wanted extra money and our parents said they'd sign the work permit papers. We left it unsaid, but we both just knew we would make better employees than the dirthead stoners we saw smoking butts out back. Even if they were sixteen.

Nic and I really got into the idea and decided it would be the coolest thing in the world to say we worked at McDonald's. We'd customize the uniforms with mod thrift store accessories. We'd wear the earrings we made out of decapitated Barbie doll heads. And most importantly, we'd only work the same shifts and never, ever eat the food. Awash with the glow of our 'alternative' mission, applications in hand, I jumped on the handlebars and Nicole pedaled us down Prospect Avenue to the Golden Arches. We walked in, handed them over to the assistant manager (who had the heavy brow of an early hominid) and headed out. The sun was setting and as Nicole rode us home, we yelled shit at cars and the kids loitering in front of Westgate Mall.

We couldn't believe that in 1985, girls and guys still had feathered hair. Of course, our personal style left much to be desired. It was sort of a combination of Salvation Army gear we'd seen the punks wearing on our trips to Berkeley (but nothing too ratty or our moms would mysteriously misplace things when they did the laundry), combined with multicolored plastic shower shoes from Woolworth's that made our feet smell really bad, and whatever Mom bought us from department stores that wasn't too geeky. We didn't quite have any one look down pat, that's what I kind of liked about us. We weren't mod or punk or goth (which at that time I think we called "new wave") or preppy. We would go to school in some of the stupidest looking outfits because we didn't care enough to have any kind of cohesive style. A typical outfit might consist of a '60s bridesmaid dress and topsiders. Or maybe camouflage pants and $90 virgin wool peach-colored Benetton sweater (Xmas present). Perhaps khaki shorts with Dad's pilfered golf shirts. Would you believe a muumuu and running shoes?

Imagine our shock when we didn't get hired. We had good GPAs! We were involved in extracurricular activities! And we were rejected by McDonald's. Our humiliation begot our big secret. We made a pact never to tell anyone that we were shut down in our quest to serve up a Happy Meal for $3.35 an hour. A couple weeks later my dad came home, Big Mac in hand, and said, "You know, they still got that 'Help Wanted' sign at

McDonald's. Didn't you turn in your application a long time ago?" But I just couldn't bring myself to follow-up. By that time, we realized that working at McDonald's would have been the all-time low of first jobs. So I waited until I was sixteen and obtained genuinely freaky employment. At a plastic surgeon's office.

Nicole called me up and said that her step-dad, who was an orthodontist, had a pal named Dr. Jellinek who needed help around the office. Nicole was going to be gone that summer so she offered the job to me. One of my main tasks was to put away polaroid photos of the patients in the correct files. There was what they called a 'surgery suite' in the office. This meant that for most of the minor stuff (liposuction, breast enlargement, collagen injections) they could do it right there. Huge light blue plastic garbage bags full of flesh would be carted out by the O.R. nurse right in front of my eyes. Best of all, every patient had a before and after photo, which made working there kind of like an endless daytime talk show where the topic was always makeovers.

Here's Mr. Carlisle before he got the fat sucked out of his chin. Here he is afterwards. See how he's smiling in the after picture. The bruises? They'll disappear shortly. He feels ten years younger and has shaved off the beard he once wore as a mask of shame.

Take a look at poor Mrs. Lewis. She lost 165 pounds and now she has what we call an 'apron' of skin hanging off of her middle section. You can't even see her pubic region, that thing is so long. We cut it right off. She can fit into her favorite spandex shorts now.

See sad, balding George Lowell. We're gonna slice into his head and stretch the skin from the parts where there's still hair growing over the patches of his classic M.P.B. or Male Pattern Baldness.

One day my humble life as high school sophomore collided with the surreal world of cosmetic surgery. Her name was Pat Gallagher and she was the Martha Stewart of the P.T.A. Whether it was a dance, dress-up day, pep rally, or football game, she was always hanging around looking like she was too old to be on campus, but somehow trying to fit in. Like someone from the Broadway production of *Grease*. Or the Fonz's last few seasons on *Happy Days*. She was the mom that made everybody else start to think that their parents weren't so annoying after all.

I went to the office one afternoon to discover that old Patsy had come in to see Dr. Jellinek. I was chomping at the bit. I grabbed her file and surreptitiously leafed through it as I was putting it away. As the operative report put it, she was "suffering from micromastia." As a small-breasted girl, I had learned early on what this meant: She was on her way to being pumped up with silicone. She was getting an "enhancement" as they called it. Now, I had seen photos of this procedure and even squeezed a few implants in my palms as I unpacked the boxes, but it became all the more real to me that day as Patsy Gallagher got new tits for Christmas.

I really wanted to tell someone, but somehow I had been brainwashed with this confidentiality crap. Every time I saw her at school I wanted to yell out something like, "Jenny Jones!" but of course Jenny Jones was just a weathergirl with a nice figure back then. Or when she passed I wanted to cough out the name of her evil disease, "micromastia." I kept it a secret for nearly three whole days. And then it was Christmas Eve. While me and my brothers squirmed our way through midnight mass at Sacred Heart, I spied Patsy a few pews over. She was wearing a tight, low-cut gold lamé blouse with a diamond pendant dangling down into her new and improved cleavage. As she slowly filed past us on her way back from receiving the body of Christ, I couldn't pass up the genius of this timing. The monsignor asked for a moment of silence to pray for the less fortunate and I leaned over and whispered, "Boobs by Jellinek!" at which my brother broke into one of those Huckleberry Hound cartoon laughs and was finally drowned out by a rousing rendition of *Joy to the World*.

The only experience in my year of employment at the surgery suite that rivals that day was when Dr. Skouros, another plastic surgeon who shared the office, came back from picking up the new vanity plate for his robin's egg blue Mercedes-Benz. I was sitting by the file cabinet, no doubt leafing through a new crop of polaroids, when he stormed in the office and demanded from me, "Get the stickers! Where are the goddamn stickers around here??!!"

I calmly opened up the drawer where we kept the office supplies and handed him a pack of file folder labels.

"This is all we have," I said.

He thrust them back at me and screamed, "Cut them up! Cut them up into little dots! I need three little dots of sticker!"

At this point, the receptionist came in and asked him what was wrong. It seems in his quest for the perfect, cheeky personalized license plate he had overlooked the basic rules of phonetics.

He explained, "I go to pick up the car and the little punk says to me, 'You must be a faggot.' I say, 'No, I am a medical doctor!' And he says, 'Well, what are you, a butt doctor? A doctor who looks up people's asses for a living?' "

Apparently the new plates on his car, plates that were supposed to translate as 'For Beauty See Me', but squeezed into the seven character limit read '4 BUT CME' or roughly 'For Butt Come'.

I followed him out to the parking lot where he stood over me as I knelt on the pavement. I arranged and rearranged little dots of sticker but was unsuccessful in disguising to the rest of the world from what an asshole he really was.

# PEAR

The rain has been coming down in sheets for three days, waterlogging the homeless and addicted on 16th Street like nerf footballs and filthy stuffed bears.

I escape for lunch from the job where all day long I fax those faxes, answer that phone, open this mail and copy, copy, copy. I am both the reigning queen of the Toshiba BD 9240 copy machine and at the same time the court jester with bedhead, runny nose, a wrinkly three-dollar dress, and for the first time in my life, corns, not calluses, but corns that cannot be cured by over-the-counter medicated pads. Another day of:

"Lorn, we've got Jim on the phone.

"Just a second, Jim. Lorn's already on the phone.

"How about Heather, can you talk to Heather? No, not your assistant Heather. Lorn's assistant, Heather. Your assistant is Heather, too? Hold on.

"Heather, I'm going to put Heather through.

"Hi, Heather. I'm going to have you talk to Heather. Heather, this is Heather. Heather, this is Heather. Okay, you Heathers talk now. Bye."

Instead of fries and a KitKat, I delude myself and have lunch at a French creperie. Just to pretend that I don't have a job. After an hour, I'm starting to think I'm not me, I'm my housemate who's writing that screenplay and can somehow (trust fund!) eat $5 bowls of French Onion everyday.

I start to leave when Daniel and Willie from the Sassoon Salon give me their cards and say I must come to the model call at the salon that evening.

They say they will correct my color, even out my skin tone, put me in a fashion show, and give me a new hairstyle that is pure genius.

"It's genius," Willie says. "Daniel is so genius."

"Stop," says Daniel.

"No, you stop, thing."

"No, you stop."

"You stop."

"You stop."

They go back and forth until they crescendo into "STOP!" give each other a poorly executed high five, and tell me to meet them at six.

So I go back to work.

"Okay, I'll fax it right over. No, I got your fax and now I'm faxing back and they're going to fax back again after Mark e-mails Tim. He's got to reach him by paging Julie or calling Stacey on her cell phone so change your 2:00 to 1:00 and your lunch to drinks cause you have a meeting about this thing from that place with whathisname and he's bringing his assistant, Heather."

I glide through the glass doors of the salon and am greeted by Daniel who kisses me on the cheek, takes me by the hand and announces, "Look at the one I found. I found this one at the creperie."

The stylists erupt into applause and all the other girls, in various stages of cut and color, give me the twice over. There are two topics of conversation: cellulite, which after much debate and *Cosmo* quoting, the group concludes is genetic; and modelling agencies. "My looks are too exotic for Stars. I've got to find someone. I'm not getting any younger. In just six months, I'll be 22."

I am bleached to a ninth level blond, given PB number 7 toner, and four hours later I am the perfect shade of cognac champagne with a style ingeniously called the Graduated Box Bob with Disconnection and Baby Doll Fringe. My makeup is pure '80s. The word in the salon is that the '80s are back. I get a *Blade Runner*esque application of white powder, black lipstick, and raccoon eyes the size of Oreos.

We are all walking around, fifteen of us, looking like rejects from a space age Robert Palmer video, when the two clothing designers single me out.

"You're a little hippy, aren't you?" one says.

And I don't get it. Maybe when I was nineteen there was that summer I lived with six housemates and ate this chili with soya gluten and we had a pet ferret...

And then I realize everyone is staring at my ass.

"I mean you're hippy. You've got hips. (Sigh.) What dress are we going to put her in, Heather?"

And Heather answers, "We could use that one that the other pear-shaped girl was going to wear."

"Where's the other pear?" Daniel asks, trying to be a helper.

I pretend to go look for her, like I had pear radar, and could home in on those whopping 36-inchers. Is she also a disgruntled gal friday with a bad attitude and a Protestant work ethic? I take off through the mirrored hallways of the salon, frightening myself at every turn, looking for my soulmate, the pear.

I storm through the glass doors until I have reached the street where I start sliding on soaking wet pavement.

# PEOPLE PLEASER

The night before last night, after drinking with co-workers who became sloppy and abusive, I almost plowed down a wall-eyed junkie whore with my truck.

She remained inches from my grill, screaming, while doing a strange shuffling jig on a pair of those plastic cha-cha spikes that make your toes, all pressed up against the clear polyurethane, look like a jar of pickled pig knuckles at the convenience store checkout. The rest of her body was barely visible in the 2 a.m. Chinatown fog, so I just stared at the dancing feet trapped in my headlights and the red O of her mouth as it released the vacant screams of a pre-teen runaway slasher movie stand-in, while I, still in the middle of the intersection, peered through my grimy windshield waiting for her to stop.

"You almost killed me, man," she said running over to my rapidly escalating driver's side window. "You owe me a ride to the BART station..." She looked a little closer. "Oh, you're a girl. Well, you're still taking me to the BART station."

She stutter-stepped back in front of my car over to the passenger's side and this was the point when I would have taken off on any other night, could have taken off down the empty street and should have taken off, but didn't. Instead, I reached over and unlocked the door. She hopped in like an overanxious prom date and started from the beginning.

Born to the owners of a coffee shop. Dad was the cook and mom was the waitress. She started washing dishes at nine and knew the value of the American dollar. I glance over at her face, a plucked chicken of a face reflecting pale, pale green from the dashboard lights.

"I'm a real people person," she says. "I like people. In high school I used to volunteer to visit this old Norwegian guy in the afternoons. Watch out! Shit!"

I swerve around two people pushing shopping carts and instantly infer from the bright lights and large trailers that these are not real homeless people, but extras in the new Don Johnson TV series. She continues on.

"The old man Sig, short not for Sigmund but for Sigurd...," she spells it out for me, "S-I-G-U-R-D." I guess Sigurd made her cut up his food into more easily digestible chunks, dispose of his disposable diapers, and read him the good bits from *People* magazine.

"I'm really a people person," she says. "So I went to L.A. and tried to get into acting, but it's all messed up down there. I had to strip and wait tables and I got a couple of parts. Hey, you know that Michael Douglas movie where he plays the whiny macho asshole?"

We're at a stoplight and I'm thinking... *Falling Down. Basic Instinct. Fatal Attraction. Wall Street. Disclosure. War of The Roses. Coma.*

"Yeah," I say.

"There's a part, right after the scene where they have the big fight and he tortures her and they have great sex and she calls him Daddy. Right after that part, there's me. I'm like standing on the corner? And I swear to God, if you look over, you can see him check me out. Michael Douglas checked me out! And I asked this guy who holds the script, the scriptholder I think he's called, if that was written down anywhere, like does it say, "Dude checks out girl on corner"? And it doesn't! Anywhere! It's like he just did it on his own ...cause he wanted to!"

I pulled up in the bus zone to drop her off and apologize. "Sorry I almost ran you down. I've had really bad luck lately."

She chews off a fingernail, spits it into her palm, looks at it, and then flicks it on the seat as she gets out saying, "Hey! Having bad luck is better than having no luck at all."

## CHRISTMAS IN TEEVEE LAND

The signs in the elevator remind me. Mass email alerts remind me. A stream of group voicemail reminds me.

The headphoned receptionist asks if I'm going. Javier who installs my sliding keyboard tray asks if I'm going. The Vice President of Sales asks if I'm going. Finally when a voice in the next bathroom stall asks if I'm going, I start shouting, "Yes! No! I don't know! How many free drinks do we get again?"

The office is buzzing today. People are leaving their desks early to get their looks together. It is the day of the Office Christmas Party. It is the adult equivalent of the senior prom except no one does coke anymore. It is the adult equivalent of the senior prom except no one will pass out in Barry Politi's parents' jacuzzi this time. They all have jacuzzis of their own to go home to.

For me the office party used to mean make something from the Moosewood cookbook, trot it over to the boss's house, and drink yeasty homebrew out of an old peanut butter jar. But somehow through a series of buyouts, mergers, downsizing, rightsizing, venture capitalism, and too many white guys named Steve, I am now employed by a television station.

I have nothing against television. I even own a television set. I don't know exactly where it came from, but it sits in my living room and I can sort of get decent reception if I drag the guitar string that's attached to the back around to the side, rub my cat against a balloon and make her lay down on it.

I think television can make you smarter. I wish someone from *The New Yorker* would write a comprehensive essay about television from which I could throw around quotations to support my claim. Somehow I know it's true.

The problem is not the television. The problem is the people who work in television. The problem is women in Bebe suits with Jennifer Aniston hair who get their tips on business from Amanda Woodward. The problem is men with perpetually close shaves and voices like baked brie saying they thought the Carnie Wilson show would be a big hit. The problem is people who call *Days of Our Lives* simply *Days*.

I end up at the party dressed like Karen Black in *Come Back To The Five and Dime, Jimmy Dean, Jimmy Dean* and I'm not sure why, sure why. I head for the bar as the hoary all-purpose wedding band (called Hot Ice or Firestorm or Rainmaker or Party Central) are churning through the high energy no-brainers of yesterdecade. The weatherman goes nuts for *Celebration*. Hell, everybody goes nuts for *Celebration*. Except me. What is wrong with me? Why can't I let go and do the bone-monkey-dookie-drop-freak-freak with a pile of newscasters at Christmas?

And as I look around the room at hundreds of urban professionals cutting loose on the parquet, the only thing I can think is, "What are they showing on Channel 4 right now? Who is minding the store?"

# WEEKEND WARRIOR

He has gone where few men have gone before. Engaged in battle, mired in strife. He is a warrior. A weekend warrior.

Careening toward the millennium, clad only in a lycra blend and a fistful of gloppy hair gel, he has found his calling. He's not gonna be one of those losers who works fifty hours a week, goes home to creditors on the phone, Mormons at the door, fence needs painting, wife wants another foot massage - not him - because he is adventurous. In high school he was the all-state tight end and runner-up for homecoming king. He was the one who organized Senior Sneak Day where they all ditched school and went to the boardwalk. That was his idea! And now ten years later, post-college, frat buddies all married and sober, he was working at a large semiconductor corporation, making decent money, living in a condo at La Rinconada. He had a cute Salvadoran girl come in once a week and clean.

Sometimes he took her to dinner and bought her dresses.

But something was wrong, dreadfully wrong. He had begun having slight anxiety attacks, shortness of breath, and the feeling that everything was caving in. It was three months away from his class reunion and somehow through the filter of the Silicon Valley sun, he was ready to make a change. Instead of sitting in front of the boob tube this weekend, watching the game and eating microwaveable spicy pepperoni hot pockets, he would tape the game instead and watch it later, fast forwarding through the commercials, because he was a busy man.

Now, he wasn't the sharpest tool in the shed, but his parents taught him to embrace the power within. He decided to seek out an extracurricular activity to set him apart from the crowd. He took up bungee jumping, skydiving, hangliding, rockclimbing, and kickboxing. With his hefty paychecks he began to load up on equipment. He acquired a kayak, water skis, tents, fishing poles, rock climbing gear, a mountain bike, a touring bike and three hundred feet of nylon cord. Cord was always useful. He now had more equipment than any of his work pals combined. Sure, Ted over in accounting had just bought that new sailboat, he thought, but Ted was bald! He had once read on a bumper sticker - He Who Dies With the Most Toys Wins - and almost ran himself off the freeway howling with laughter. And you always wondered who laughed at bumper stickers.

You always wondered who found meaning in the idiotic pop-psychology of a Suzuki Samurai cruising down the freeway with placards stuck on its ass proclaiming identity snippets for the boob who shelled out thousands on an aqua piece of plastic. I am important! I am an American original, man! I walked into Payless to get disposable razors and a case of my favorite red, white and blue decaffeinated beverage and found myself right there on the rack! I cheered myself on, "Woo-hoo!" doing the impersonation of Homer Simpson that always makes me the life of the party, debating the additional purchase for a strip mall second, before I plunked down the bread for a piece of me. I belong. I have a sense of humor. Bumper stickers speak to me:

Get in, shut up and hold on.

As a matter of fact, I do own the whole damn road.

If you don't like the way I drive, stay off the sidewalk.

Fahvernugen Fuckengruven.

Mean People Suck, Nice People Swallow.

Jesus is Love. Jesus is Lord. Jesus is my best friend. God is my co-pilot.

My other car is an airplane. My other car is a horse. My other car is in my four car garage while my wife is being orally serviced by the pool boy!

I will take the extra time to personalize my means of automotive transportation. I will be the master of my commute from the 17 to the 880 to the 280 to the 101. I am more smug than the president of the Hair Club for Men and Paul at The Diamond Center combined because I am a weekend warrior.

# THE HAPPIEST PLACE

Since I quit my job, the happiest place on earth is in my sneakers as I'm riding my beater Schwinn past Dee Dee Doll House Hair Salon and Flint's BBQ on my way to the post office at 2:30 in the afternoon.

After waking up at noon, I went to Peet's Coffee where the employees were eyeing me with suspicion. I know this look. This is the way that I used to eye all the slackers slacking along Valencia during my one hour -no more no less- lunch break where I'd grab a burrito and head back to my cubicle. I didn't have time to buy, sell or trade clothing at the vintage store, no time to stop by the listening station at the record shop, no time for an herbal facial peel, no time to sample soy cheeses at Whole Foods. I was a prisoner of the phone and the fax and the email and the meetings and the sales figures and the press releases and the cheesy promo photos of insolent comedians playing at Cobb's Comedy Club.

There's a long line at the post office. Now, I haven't been inside a post office for about six years. I could just run things through the meter at the office. So all of a sudden, I feel like Princess Di after the divorce. You know, doing real people tasks and being filled with amazement and wonder about the realness of it all. There are sixteen people in line and one woman behind the counter. Well, there are actually four women behind the counter. One is working. Two are animatedly going over a recipe for fat-free butterscotch chip pan cookies and one is snacking on said pan cookie.

This is making everyone very irritated. Not me. I've got nowhere to be. I didn't park at a meter. I'm not sneaking in on the way back from a dentist appointment planning ahead to complain to my coworkers about how long they always make me wait there. I am having a great time listening to the woman ahead of me complain loudly. "This is ridiculous! Look at them back there. We'd all be better off if we couldn't see that they were there at all. They don't care. They just don't care." The new age lady in back of me is sighing repeatedly and at very short intervals. At one point I think she is going to hyperventilate, she is sighing so much.

Then he walks to the window. A physically fit grandpa type who's been nodding along the whole time, interjecting, "Yup. You betcha. No sense of pride in their work." We're all listening closely because there's nothing else to do now that we've already read every piece of text on the posters for the unveiling of the new limited addition Heroes of Rhythm and Blues collector stamps. At least five more people have joined the line. Many more have walked in, looked around bewildered, and walked out dejectedly with their packages. They apparently sensed that a post office filled with twenty-odd seething customers conveying sheer hatred with their body language and a handful of postal workers chewing on olestra-laced goodies was the last place they want to be when the apocalypse hit.

So Grandaddy gets up there. Slowly, he pulls something out of his pocket and says, "Do I need a special envelope for this?" The postlady says, "Well, yeah. I guess you could buy one of the padded kind. For a dollar."

He replies, "Yeah. Cause it's metal and I didn't think I could just put that in a regular envelope."

We're all craning our necks to see what he's got. It looks just about the size of a large paper clip or the metal tab on a sodapop can. And then I realize that it is the metal tab from a sodapop can. So, I'm guessing that it's some sort of contest. You mail in the tabs and maybe you win tickets to the Superbowl. (My brother later confirmed this.)

And my mind starts reeling. My mind has not been sent reeling this fast since I bought a faux fur cavewoman mini dress at a garage sale for a quarter. A quarter! Hand sewn with a matching cavewoman shoulder wrap and everything.

This man has been waiting in line for at least a half hour with a (yes, "a" meaning "one") Coca Cola pop tab in his warm little sweatpants pocket. Don't feel sorry for him. He wasn't one of those seniors from the group home where they bring in cats once a week for them to hold and then take them away and all week long they say stuff like, "Those kitties sure were cute. When are they bringing the kitties back? Tuesday? ...When's Tuesday?"

He was a good looking former high roller sugar daddy Adam West type. And he was entering a little contest put on by the Coca Cola Corporation. On a Thursday at 3 p.m. So he's just like me. Nothing better to do than stand in line at the post office.

But on so many levels, I am confused. Why the special envelope? Can you not mail a pop tab in a regular five cent envelope? As a matter of fact, aren't you supposed to be able to put the correct postage on anything and it will be delivered? Like the cigarette butts the artists sent to Jesse Helms, and the maxi pads the feminists sent to Ronald Reagan? He probably could have put a stamp on that pop tab and every postal worker in the United States would send that thing to the Coca Cola headquarters. Like the miracle deliveries that just say Santa or God or Regis Philbin or something. I think it would be completely wrong, and may I venture downright un-American, for one of the largest conglomerates on the planet to hold a contest where everyone had to purchase a one dollar padded ledger size envelope to enter? Okay, so maybe he was playing it smart. They're going to get millions of those plain white regulation envelopes in the contest department. His will stand out. He's done a lot of thinking about this. Some may say too much thinking. But not me.

While the annoyance of the people in line now shifts away from the postal employee over to the old guy as he pays for the envelope with a fifty, gets his change counted out to him dollar by dollar, as he recounts his bills to make sure they're all there, carefully closes wallet, unbuttons his back pocket to insert wallet, as he declines her offer for a little baggie to put the pop tab in, as he slowly hand letters the address WHILE STILL AT THE COUNTER, while he tries licking the envelope closed even though it has a self-adhesive strip, I am content to stand in no one else's sneakers but mine and dissect everything that crosses my path one Thursday afternoon at a time.

THE HOMEOWNER'S ASSOCIATION VOTED TO REPLACE THE SIGNS FOR THE NEIGHBORHOOD CUL-DE-SACS . . . THEY WOULD NOW SAY NOT A THROUGH STREET INSTEAD OF DEAD END.

## REACHING FOR PORK

We are lined up at the hostess stand. Five minutes and counting until the all-you-can-eat Mother's Day brunch buffet is officially open. Herding into the doorway at an establishment that calls itself 'A Class Act' right on the menu, everyone is anxiously clasping their coupons. A steaming slab of beef goes by and the family in front of us shuts up fast.

"What a lovely roast," someone whispers. Dad in Dockers, Junior in skater clothes from the skater clothes department of Mom's favorite discount store, Little Miss Pre-teen doing her interpretation of *Sassy* magazine's latest spread on developing your own signature style no matter what the popular kids say, and Mom. With corsage on the shiny gold 49ers jacket and sneakers embedded with rhinestones, she reels around cause she's the reeling kind and hits my mom square in the face with her padded shoulder. Football Fan Mom doesn't even apologize.

"Are you okay?" I ask my mom and pat her on the head. The woman's husband hears this, grabs his wife's elbow, looks squarely at my dad and says, "Watch it, buddy" as if Dad just copped a feel off her stretchpanted ass. For a second I swear a fight is going to break out, but then the hostess - all gooey lips and heavy eyeliner - releases the silver rope and families hurtle into the banquet room, heads lolling about, lower lips slack with wonder.

Standing in line for custom omelettes, a chubby ten-year-old keeps jostling me with her plate of iceberg lettuce, telling her sister, "I'm on a diet. I'm only eating salad. I saw it on TV." She plucks a sausage from the chafing dish and puts it straight in her mouth. "I'm only counting once we sit down at the table, though." The line passes her by as she licks her fingers and reaches for pork.

# THINGS YOU PUT IN A JAR

"You cannot see, smell or taste botulism," says Aunt June with a voice like Knute Rockne's. "You can only destroy molds and yeast by boiling to 212 degrees. But for the destruction of bacteria," she slams her palm down on the formica for emphasis, "you gotta ride it up to 240."

It is late August and I'm jarring things with my Aunt June. We're just putting things in jars right there in Pekin, Illinois. As the legend goes, they named the town Pekin because it was thought to lie on the same latitudinal line as Peking, China. This was later discovered to be false, but they were so set on associating themselves with something more exotic - something besides just saying "we're right outside of Peoria" - that they named the high school basketball team the Chinks anyway. This was later discovered to be rather unsavory, so in the '70s they changed it to the Dragons. "That's still kind of Oriental," the mayor said.

At 8:30 in the morning, having risen, shone, and eaten our biscuits and gravy, I am sweating like a pig and June is glistening like a pistol. Her hands are gripping jars, her forearms are tightening lids, and her upper arms are moving wherever the hell they please while her sleeveless housedress plays a hit parade of daisies and gladioli. We're only about an hour into the whole project and I am already starting to lag. Though I have consumed four cups of coffee, I know I have only been administered as much caffeine as half a cup of Peet's. The phrase "there has to be a Starbuck's around here somewhere" actually pops into my mind and I am ashamed.

June snaps me out of it by giving me the rundown of things you put in a jar. "You got yer jellies, jams, preserves, conserves, marmalades and butters. And don't forget the picklers like pickalilli, chow-chow and tutti frutti."

Aunt June pops a couple of Alka-Seltzer in a glass of water.

"Land," she says patting her chest. "I like to say 'em almost as much as I like to eat 'em."

She sings her way through a new composition where all the words are "pickalilli, chow-chow and tutti frutti." I try to join in but everything I sing sounds like the melody to *Top of the World* by The Carpenters.

# BLANKATHON

Uncle Lou, you used to ride your hawg down the Pacific Coast Highway in 1974. Your hair was long, your beard was full, and those tattoos were fresh, legible. You were shooting up, up into the stars, hanging on one just for a second before spiraling down, down, down to your smelly duplex in Van Nuys that you shared with your infected girlfriend who along with your infected babies cruised around the L.A. freeways in the beat-up Honda donated to you by your eighteen-year-old nephew, the psych major, who was upgrading his vehicle.

Sweet shy Michael. You were always called a faggot by the jocks. But you came out in style, transformed, going to underwear parties in West Hollywood. Giving Sandra Bernhard a lift home to her place in the Valley. She was such a bitch. Got into your car and said, "It smells in here." You had thirty-four pairs of shoes and a loom in your living room. You learned how to weave.

Kisses, bites, secretions, conspiracies of biological warfare. There's a walkathon, jog-a-thon, dance-a-thon, bike-a-thon, bake sale. Orange currant scones for research.

The wedding in the Castro where all the signs used to designate parking mistakenly said 'Funeral', and somebody's mom from Pleasanton or Pleasant Valley or Pleasant Hill, she was pleasant, not meaning any harm, just making casual conversation with another wedding guest, said, "Ohmigod, this is a riot. They accidentally put out the wrong signs. Somebody get a picture of the bride and groom in front of the funeral signs. Photo op!"

And this sparse-haired guy, all splotchy with sarcoma, trips over her Louis Vuitton bag on his way into the rec center to play bingo and drink donated juice.

And we're having ourselves a real Time-Life, Associated Press, Kodak moment. The smiling bride and groom, the fallen victim of infectious disease, all framed in the shadow of Most Holy Redeemer Church. And I thank the lucky star Lou still hangs off of, that everyone had the presence of mind not to take out their cameras and shoot.

## EMPRESS OF SIGHS

Mom and Dad have abandoned the family home and retired to Palm Desert. They moved into one of those gated communities of steel framed homes on Gerald Ford between Date Palm and Bob Hope. Just cross the intersection of Frank Sinatra and the Gene Autry Trail near the corner of Fred Waring and Phil Harris, who for all the kids under 50 was a big bandleader married to a big movie star whose name no one can quite remember anymore, except she used to drink with Lucille Ball in her pjs at Fletcher's and died a mess. Who doesn't anymore?

Mom says getting there is a snap, as easy as a cake falling off a log. Just take a left on Palm Canyon until you reach Desert Falls, bear left at the fork of Indian Canyon and Canyon Plaza taking Desert Canyon to Canyon Sands. This is where you find Rancho La Paz. Click on 2 for the gate, the guard waves you past and you're on Avenida del Sol where you continue on crossing Vista del Sol, Plaza del Sol, Vista del Monte, Sunny Dunes, Camino Parocela - make sure you heed the golf cart crossing - and then Thousand Palms, Emerald Desert, Desert Isle and Palm Desert Greens. Left on Sagewood, right on Sungate, left on Palo Verde, and ending in the cul de sac of Casa La Paz.

"I just love it," Mom says.

"You love it?" I say.

"Yes. I love it!" Then she calls to dad who's enjoying himself on the eighteen-hole putting green located just three feet outside the kitchen sliding glass door, "Don't we love it, hon?"

He tips the brim of his white cap, a cap he would have seen on someone a year ago and called them a fag, and says, "Love it! Another crappy day in paradise! Ha! Ha! Ha!"

Mom clears her throat a little and sighs. She is the Empress of Sighs. "Well, yes, it's still a little funny."

Same funny tax bracket, same funny year round tans, same funny cathedral ceilings. Same cars, same stocks, same paranoia and medication. Same politics and annoying anal polyps.

The same leather interior, glossy exterior and liposuctioned posterior.

Here comes the neighbor driving up in a luxury sedan just like your luxury sedan except he paid extra for the little headlight wipers and the gold linked license plate frame — and you didn't. You thought they were useless, extraneous, a little much... and now your neighbor comes rubbernecking by, waving real slow, doing the grown-up equivalent of "Ha-ha!" which is basically "Ha-ha! I am worth more than you."

And Mom sighs and admits it doesn't feel like home yet. This mom, Empress of Sighs, empress of afterschool treats and frumpy sweaters and marathon tickling and the *52 Casseroles* cookbook, doesn't feel at home.

So I map out a plan. I make a list on how one feels at home here. I say, you need to play bridge, throw a party, plan on some tennis, and it'll feel like home. Polish the silver, throw out old photos, balance your checkbook, it'll feel like home. Start eating more fresh fruit. Get your armpits waxed. Drink six 8 oz. glasses of water each day. It'll feel like home. Squeeze all your blackheads, clip your toenails in bed, watch thirteen straight hours of television. Complain about what trash they show on television and start writing a letter. Stop writing the letter cause it makes you think about yourself, yell at your mother instead, quit drinking, go on a crying jag, threaten to deport the gardener.

Consider rhinoplasty, blepharoplasty, and tummy tuck. Forget to water the plants. Buy plastic plants and forget to dust them. Buy bananas and watch them rot. Buy books and pretend you read them. Start a collection. Start a collection of something that might be worth something someday.

Now turn off the lights, sprawl out on one of the matching earthtoned leather sofas and pick a very high number. Start counting backwards. You're in the middle of the desert, the wind picks up and when you run out of numbers, you will find that it feels a lot like home.

## LONG WEEKEND

Did he ever wind up marrying that little Oriental gal?

75 degrees at Christmas. This is why we live in California.

She already decided when she walked into that car dealership that she was coming out with a new car and a new husband.

There's a cute starter condo for sale just around the corner.

Why don't you ask him at the New Year's Eve party whether you should sell all of your shares yet?

You don't need the city. We've got it all right here.

This used to be a real famous place where all the movie stars came. The owner was gay, but he could really pack 'em in here.

This show isn't so great. We only watch it cause it comes on right after our favorite program.

It's a really easy appetizer. You just need a couple different kinds of cheese and some mayonnaise. Spread it on little toast triangles and melt it in the oven.

Our floor plans are exactly the same. Except flip-flopped.

None of these recipes make use of the Osterizer. I think this book was written before they even invented the Osterizer.

We just use the whites on account of the cholesterol.

They're drunk by 11:30 a.m. That's why I decided to take over as the earthquake monitor for our block.

It had to be the housekeeper. Nobody else had the keys.

After a second hip replacement you might actually need one of those Niagara adjustable beds.

We better turn in. We have breakfast club tomorrow at 8:00.

# CRAPPY BROWN CARPETING

Crappy brown carpeting never felt so good
S-A-T-U-R-D-A-Y Night
And I'm laying on it
smoking cigarettes and doing push-ups on it
Cracking my back, talking really loud to myself
Checking out my new bruises and burns on it
Saturday night

Lights on, lights off
TV on, TV off
Music on, music off
Heat on, heat off
Open the windows, close the windows
Cook up some scrambled eggs, rinse off a fork

and I'm right back to it

Crappy brown carpeting
I'm eating my dinner on it
Crapping brown carpeting
I am living in it

The freelance graphic designer's housewarming party should be
in full swing right about now

Polished hardwood floors, Persian rugs, avant garde bathroom fixtures
just the right jazz
and the Crate & Barrel martini set displayed on the sideboard but
everyone's just drinking a middle-of-the-road chardonnay

Bistro owners, journalists, people with PhDs, studio musicians
and that girl Darcy who's so close to her sharpei Micki, she says,
"We even get our period on the same day."
An opera singer
A party with a real live opera singer

Now I could have taken a shower, finally combed out my hair
Put on a black dress, got in my truck, found the place,
gone up the walkway, rang the bell, but you know what?
Somebody would have answered it

And then there would have been a drink
Thank you very much
Fake laughter, ha ha
Small talk
I'm Beth. I am a baker.

And then me breaking a glass or tucking my dress into my nylons
Exposing my flank at yet another party

Maybe if I was lucky I would have met an old guy
who would financially support me in exchange for something harmless
like gardening in the nude, but I wasn't banking on it

The only thing I could count on that night
was the other things that I hate so much
That I love, that I hate so much that I love
I get them so confused

*Tom Jones: Live at the Talk of the Town*
The smell of a skunk
A good cup of bad coffee

Miniature TV sets
Gigantic brandy snifters
Highway rubberneckers
Rolls of pennies
Stray whiskers
Sticky fingers
Sweaty palms

And my crappy, crappy brown carpeting

# SO LITTLE SLEEP SO FAR

Isabel had stripped down to her underwear by the time she reached the outskirts of Albuquerque. That's how hot it was at 2:00 a.m. She was both excited and surprised by her ability to maintain 65 miles per hour while pulling off her shorts and t-shirt. Now she was just wearing a pair of saggy ass cotton briefs and one of those sports bras. It bothered her for a minute that she couldn't remember how she'd acquired that lavender spandex bra. Must have been from one of those 50+ housemates in one of those sixteen group households between '87 and '94. That blonde girl, Sherry maybe? Or was her name Shelly? Jesus Christ, she thought. An endless stream of bartenders, strippers, schoolteachers, cooks, temps, trustfunders, and activists. Berkeley, Oakland, San Francisco, Santa Cruz, San Jose. They were all a blur now, the people and the places. She was glad she'd left them behind.

The backs of her thighs were hopelessly stuck to the vinyl interior of her old Plymouth Horizon. She'd been driving for the last twelve hours, keeping her mind off the heat by making up her own words to the songs on the radio. She thought she could be better than Weird Al Yankovic if she just put her mind to it. She couldn't sing that well, but she was clever with lyrics. Maybe he needed somebody to write words for him. Maybe he was too busy and famous to do all the work himself anymore. She'd look into that as soon as she got her shit together in Albuquerque. This was going to be her lucky town. She could feel it.

She peered down onto the floor of the backseat to see how her cat Buddy was doing. He was so still he looked like he was dead. She scooped him up with her right hand and shook him a little. When he barely moved, she pulled off onto the shoulder. She jumped out of the car, the scorching asphalt tearing at her bare feet, and ran around to the hatchback. She tore the case off her pillow, opened the gallon of water she had brought for her radiator and soaked the pillowcase with it. She shoved Buddy inside and started to cry. A semi was heading toward them, its headlights illuminating Isabel as she hopped around in her undies holding the limp body of her only pal. The driver blared his horn as he passed. She hated that damn Doppler Effect. It freaked her out every time. She got back in the car and clutched the pillowcase tight to her chest. After a couple minutes, she peered inside and was relieved to see Buddy looking up at her blinking.

It looked like all the motels on Route 66 had vacancies so she chose the one with the coolest sign, The Tradewinds. She pulled into a dark spot, put her clothes back on and headed toward the office. After ringing the bell for awhile, an old guy with pockmarked skin and no eyebrows appeared in his pajamas.

"Hiya, snackcake," he said. He was one of those people who made a little whistling sound with his s's. She paid for one night, determined to find a permanent place to live tomorrow.

"Sleep soundly," he whistled. "See you soon."

Isabel was sure he was doing this whistling thing on purpose. When she went back to the car to get Buddy, the pillowcase was empty. He must have jumped out the window.

The next day Isabel took a drive around to get the lay of the land. This was her town now. She thought she might start a rock band or do a radio show or something. She'd check out the scene later. Now she needed to find herself a job and a place to live. She'd find a place by midnight or it was on to the next city.

So far she'd stopped in Los Angeles, San Diego, Vegas, and Phoenix. It just seemed to her that when she finally decided to call everyone and tell them where she went, she wanted to be able to say, "It all happened in one day. Great apartment. Great job. All on my first day in town. I knew I was meant to be here."

She reasoned she could still lie and say that was how it happened even if it didn't work out that way, but she didn't want to be that pathetic. Plus, if it didn't all come together in one day, she probably wasn't in the right town. Look what happened last time. Isabel needed to give herself time restrictions. She needed to make bets with herself to prove she was on the right track. When she was a kid, she used to see if she could separate the family laundry into whites and darks and run it down to the laundry room, all without breathing. Things like this helped her tremendously.

Her afternoon was an exercise in futility. After Isabel realized she'd never be able to afford a place by herself, she started in on the dreaded shared housing search. All the houses she went to had at least one person who reminded her of a former roommate that had either ripped her off, developed a drug habit, or ended up in a mental ward.

The job hunt was no better. Optimistically, she began with her 'A list' which included bookstores, cafes, and record shops. When nothing panned out there, she went to restaurants, clothing stores, and bars with live music. Nothing. The moment Isabel found herself inquiring about a receptionist position at a 24-hour gym, she went to the movies and didn't come out until it as very dark outside.

It was nearly midnight when Isabel pulled into a parking lot. She became acutely aware of her good attitude regarding the heat, Buddy's disappearance, her relative lack of funds, and yet another city that wasn't meant for her. She wondered if being aware of maintaining a good attitude meant that she didn't really have one at all. That she was faking it. She dismissed this notion, wiped the sweat off her forehead by leaning down into her lap and wiping it on her skirt and went into a convenience store to stock up for the long drive ahead of her. She was off to Denver. Or Dallas maybe.

"Hey," she said to the guy behind the counter.

"Hey," he said without looking up from his book. He was about her age, maybe a little younger, wearing an Alka Seltzer t-shirt. He looked like a smart ass.

"So, I just got here last night," Isabel said, putting a couple bags of salty things, some candy bars, and a two liter bottle of generic cola down on the counter. "Tell me where to get a job and a place to live. In the next ten minutes." The guy looked up from his book and closed it without saving his place.

"There are no jobs in this town," he said. "Which is why I am working here. I suppose I could quit this job, because it is sooooo shitty, and then you could have it. Do you want this job? Huh? Look around! Oh, I'm sure you saw *Clerks* and thought it was really hip to work at a fucking 7-11. It's really hip! Don't I look like the ultimate scenester to you? Where's your Super 8? Let's start filming!" The corners of his mouth were getting white and gummy. "No, I do not know where you can find a job or a place to live. I am not the classified section of the paper nor is this the town square where everyone gathers to exchange nuggets of information. Do I look like the town crier to you? Or do I look like a total loser who watches too many movies and makes minimum wage? That'll be $7.49."

She looked straight at him for a long time. "Nice monologue, man," she finally said.

"Well, fuck me running!" he said in a fake hick accent.

Isabel fired fake guns at him with her fingers, Dean Martin style. She slapped eight bucks down and grabbed one of those pine tree car air fresheners on her way out.

She got all the way out to the Horizon when she heard him yelling. "Come back, you sassy sister!" He was standing there with the door open.

"I'm quitting my job and moving," he yelled across the parking lot. "In two weeks. They already hired somebody to be the counter bozo, but you can have my room if you want."

Isabel walked slowly back toward the store. "What's the housemate situation?" she asked. "Honestly."

"It's just me and my girlfriend. Ex-girlfriend actually. We have our own rooms. She's cool. She's a massage therapist."

Isabel had lived with a few massage therapists in her day and knew the pitfalls. Weird people showing up all the time. They try to get out of doing the dishes by offering massage in exchange. Inevitable bad taste in music. Weird teas.

"Let me get you a beer and I'll call Beatrice and tell her you're coming."

Isabel looked at her watch. It was past midnight. She had to keep moving, but figured she had time for one free beer.

## BABE AND THE BATHWATER

She bends over and grasps the latest issue
But it slips out of her hands on account of it being
so very glossy
Conceptualizing grasping the issue
tongue wetting lips
spit bubbles catching fluorescence

She bends over in the superstore
Checker checks out her ass
without forming a single thought
she picks up on this
and picks it up
puts down her cash

You've come a long way, baby
like an old negro spiritual she learned
in her whitewashed fourth grade classroom,
it sings to her at the checkout
You've come a long way, baby
Awaiting her sweet chariot with plush leather interior
and a lit vanity mirror
Comin' for to carry her

Later, at home, she proves handy
following instructions for an evening alone
Icing the spritzer glass
Lighting scented candles
Slipping into a warm bath with aromatherapeutic essential oils

She 'luxuriates'
    wonders for a moment if she is doing this properly
Properly asserts no negative energy invade
her special time and continues
Sloughing off dead skin cells with a loofah sea sponge
    See sponge slough - slough, sponge, slough
Methodical and circular
she works faster and faster, breaking a sweat,
covering every inch and then
repeating to make certain she's got it all

Satisfied with a job well done,
her unreasonably attractive big toe
lets down the hammer on the drain
    (she has always taken pride in her feet)
She makes tea, eats a light meal, does twenty-five butt tweezes
and jumps into bed

She clicks off the light,
    her senses reeling,
        ears ringing,
                wringing her hands
    no ring on her finger

She worries about the ring in the tub

REMEMBER THAT

IF YOU EVER BECOME A PORN STAR,

THE PERFECT STAGE NAME IS ONE CREATED FROM YOUR FIRST

FAMILY PET AND YOUR GRANDMOTHER'S MAIDEN NAME.

MINE WOULD BE APPLES CALLAHAN.

# Elegy For A
## Greedy, Slothful Orthodontist

Dr. Melvin Gunderson was my clean shaven, golf-playing, Listerine swilling, dandruff shouldered smarmy pseudo psycho ortho monstro dentist dontist. Careless with his hands, eyes darting like a pachinko game. As vile as any character created by a mother-hating method actor with trenchmouth. Yes, he was an orthodontist with bad teeth.

I met him when I was twelve. Feathered hair, tight jeans and this pink elephant sweater, the trunk extended down the sleeve. My mom bought it for me at the Lollipop Tree at the Argonaut Shopping Centre, ("Mom, *please!*") a strip mall with a Safeway and a Long's Drugs and a Hallmark Store. My groovy math teacher told me it was cool so I wore it three times a week with a pink nylon shirt underneath. It was that shimmery clingy manmade blend that makes you sweat and gives you the chills at the same time. I smelled so bad. Mom said, "Honey, you're a woman now. Here's some roll-on." But I refused to acknowledge it, my prepubescent hairless armpits went untouched, smelling like taco meat.

I didn't complain when Dr. Melvin Gunderson pounded blue plastic spacers in between my teeth to ready me for my first pair of braces. In 1981 we all had braces and never complained, visions of those Pearl Drops ads, mmmmmm. We just waited patiently as a prayer to emerge like butterflies or Cheryl Tiegs, patiently digging out clumps of wet Fritos and Sugar Daddy caramel. A short seven months later, he told me I was ready. He never gave me the retainer that I wanted so much so I made my own with paper clips and a Jolly Rancher Fire Stick. A retainer had its own little case, like the diaphragm I got later that failed and now sits in a trunk in my parents' garage preserved with a little cornstarch. It's right next to my collection of glass and ceramic mice preserved in between sheets of toilet paper and my first communion dress preserved in plastic. First communion, a white ribbon in my bowlcut and gap teeth. Teeth that were never crooked or straight, but still strong, California sun, milk drinking teeth.

A year later, trading in my Farrah Fawcett 'do for a short Olivia Newton-John accessorized with metallic headband, my teeth more crooked than ever. Dr. Gunderson put those braces right back on. It wasn't supposed to work this way. Another year of being stationwagoned to his stinking office from track practice, student council, the mall, and the houses of kids with bad grades whose parents were in Bali. And after that year, to my horror, my teeth were even worse.

Dr. Gunderson told my parents that what I really needed was gum surgery. We were on the Lockheed Missiles and Space insurance plan. It was 1983. That would cover it. Breathing shallow as a rabbit, he promised, "This time for sure."

He dosed me in the chair until I started spinning; seeing stick ponies, bald dancing marionettes, a black mousepuppy licking a bannister. He parted my lips with his fingers and sliced behind my top lip and down. He started scraping and scooping bloody tissue and then wiping it back and forth on my blue paper bib like buttering white bread. Sewing me up with black stitches, in and out, in and out, gripping my lip between thumb and forefinger.

The boys I babysat, the Chesneys, who squealed and humped my leg when I called them the Chestnuts, drew a get-well card. A mouth with only gums. *We hope your gums feel better. Smell ya later! Doug & Steve.*

As for Melvin Gunderson, someone finally hauled his skinny ass comb-over hairdoed head out of the yellowgreen couched faux wood paneled orifice office and into court, but my parents were too sensible for lawsuits.

See, Mister Melvin Gunderson was a mister that whole time, not a doctor at all. I remember he once told me as I sat helpless in his chair, his thick ungloved fingers working deep inside, "You know, little girl, your mouth heals quicker than anything."

## STUFF TO DO IN SARATOGA WHEN YOU'RE BORED

It was tough to grow up in the suburbs. For every pot-smoking hesher or combustible jock, there was a normal kid who didn't want to hang out at the mall or go to the pep rally. We had to think of other options. Like forming the Church of Chuck Woolery. My friend's sister painted a beautiful portrait of Chuck surrounded by an angelic golden glow. We'd exchange little tidbits about Chuck's life, or wonder aloud, "What would Chuck do in a situation like this?"

At the commercial break on *Love Connection* when Chuck said he'd be back in "two minutes and two seconds" - he often just flashed a grin and a peace sign and said, "Two and two" - we'd get out our watches and time it, cheering him on. Chuck was always right as rain. This entertained us for about a month. Why worship Satan when there are so many game show hosts worthy of their very own cult?

Another fun diversion was to make up fake stories and call the local newspaper. My friend Nicole held the title for this one. Without letting anyone else in on the prank, she convinced a local reporter that she rose each morning at 3 a.m. to sweep the streets of the town. She said she wanted to give something back to the community that had done so much for her. They came to her house while her parents were at work, photographed her out in the street with a push broom and ran a full page story with a 'local teens aren't all bad' type of angle. The congratulatory letters came pouring in from her former teachers and various senior citizens. And of course, the kids at school decided she was even weirder than they thought.

The local 7-11 was the place to find out where the parties were. Sometimes you didn't even have to pull into the parking lot. You could just hear some thick-necked jock bellowing "Off Sobey Road, dude!" out of his Bronco over to the big-hair girls in the Mazda RX-7. We'd follow behind, in our humble wood-paneled stationwagon, park far away from the house, and then commando around the yard until we found an open door or window. We'd sneak inside, find a room that no one was in, hide out, and eavesdrop. There is nothing like the scintillating conversation of girls with mohair sweaters and sticky lipgloss drinking wine coolers. Or guys in too-tight jeans, big L.L. Bean sweaters, desert boots, and denim jackets with sheepskin collars pounding Bud after Bud bragging about who they are having sex with while their parents are out of town.

We played board games on the roof of the bank downtown. This was also a good spot to watch our favorite student couples get in fights as they left local restaurants.

We wore wigs and frumpy sweatsuits, and drank four or five pots of coffee at Denny's. This once led us to flesh out a crude musical about Denny's. All the songs were composed on napkins and sugar packets. We had vignettes about greasy ladyfingers, Grand Slam breakfasts, and our favorite employees like Joseph, the ex-military computer student, and Bib, the grandmother of nine.

We scaled the foothills and snuck in to see the shows during the Paul Masson Winery Summer Concert Series. We never got caught. Who would ever suspect teenagers of breaking the law to scope out Sergio Mendez or Smokey Robinson? By purchasing one $30 ticket and hiding people in the trunk, drive-in movie style, we also got to see James Brown, Ray Charles and Ella Fitzgerald.

We didn't boycott the prom because it was stupid. You had to check it out at least once. We brought a large watermelon and danced only with it during the slow songs. For the fast songs, we dragged one of the parent chaperones out on the floor and went crazy. We didn't just play air guitar. We played air keyboards and air saxophone. Attached toilet paper to our shoes and pretended not to understand why everyone was making fun of us. Asked Mr. Suave if he wanted a cigar and then put a Tampax in his breast pocket. Stepped back and enjoyed his reaction as he was disgusted at the thought of retrieving a paper-wrapped piece of cotton. (For the older set, this also works in retro nightclubs!)

We would go to Safeway and rearrange the displays. The best one was the Healthy Heart display. Item by item, we replaced the oat bran muffins, apples, and black beans until underneath the huge sign that read 'Make Your Heart Healthy and Happy' was an exhibit of cigarettes, bourbon, bologna, and Ding Dongs.

This is just a small sampling of ways we dealt with teenage suburban existence. And if I can help even one kid survive until graduation, I'll feel that I have made a difference. Go Falcons!

# DEVIL'S VACATION

The five hour flight to Cabo San Lucas. It was a vacation offered to me kind of like a doggie bag from Tony Roma's or Stuart Anderson's Black Angus. You know, higher end fast food fare, leftover, didn't cost nothing, take it or leave it, but I'd take it if I were you, girl, cause you're going nowhere fast.

I just wanted to sleep the sleep of an honest woman. So when the stewardess leaned in close and breathed into my ear, "Here. Put this stir stick in your drink," I didn't pay much attention to her. It wasn't until I looked into her eyes I could see that she was as tired of this, as tired of all of this, as I was. "Somehow," she said, her face really close to mine, "the stick keeps the drink from spilling during turbulence. I'm not a physicist. I don't know why. Just do it."

Well, my drink spilled anyway and that might have been my fault, but for a moment we had something, she and I. We had made a connection aboard this party-bound flying machine. And yells of "Cabo! Right on, Cabo, dude!" were already escaping the wet tequila lips of other passengers as we soared high above the border and she tried to accommodate each and every one of us as best as she knew how. I tried to make eye contact with her as I deplaned, so I could say "Bye! Thanks for the stir-stick tip!" but she was busy picking something out of her shoe and didn't notice me.

I felt for her. She should not have this job. A real human should not have this job. They should just start breeding gals that will never go above a hundred and thirty, whose feet won't swell and implants won't leak. See, kids could barf on them, assholes could pinch them, men over fifty could insult the cooking like it was their own homemade recipes they were serving up. Why not? They're already breeding those crusty pilots with the smoky, sleepy voices, and that special brand of poultry with extra fatty lobes hanging off that can just be snipped in perfect two ounce servings. They are breeding those tall, healthy, perfectly tan kids who flock to Cabo Wabo, the nightclub owned by Van Halen (hey! is that Eddie and Valerie?). They go a little nuts, get a little crazy, get away from it all cause they deserve it, don't they? And every night when *Monie Monie*, the Billy Idol version, comes on, and it always does... at that part in between verses, that part where my mother used to furiously dance the frug, these kids are chanting:

"Everybody party! Get laid! Get fucked"

*Monie Monie*

"Everybody party! Get laid! Get fucked!"

They're just grinding, dry humping, interlocking those neon crotches and feeling, if only for a week, a little bit nasty. Boy, those kids from San Diego are all over it and wasn't San Diego supposed to be the next Seattle? I mean, after Portland and Austin and Chapel Hill? The look on their faces is saying, "Woo! Dancing it doggie-style is equal opportunity now!" The look on their faces says that somebody forgot to tell these kids that sex doesn't really shock anymore, that the only thing we all got left is murder. And we are breeding killers like we are breeding sports fans, Winona-bes, whiskey dick uncles, and cynical bitches, who relapse occasionally, and attempt to make connections with flight attendants.

# *Fix*

I am speaking the truth when I say that I was lonely. I was lonely, lonely, desperately lonely. I didn't plan any way out of it. It just started happening real slow, see?

I began by lingering a little, fingering the little palm of the grocery clerk handing me my receipt. Doing things like forcing my locked gazes on toll takers, meter maids, cops, dry cleaners, and pizza delivery boys. I would pace myself as I walked the streets so I'd deliberately collide with strangers and then I could apologize, "Hey, I'm sorry. Do you have change for a dollar?" when I didn't need change at all.

But I needed change because I was lonely and things weren't working out like I planned. I didn't plan this. These chance encounters, they were just chance encounters, weren't the way to meet people. So to meet people, I started going to meetings.

I skipped A.A., A.C.A., N.A., incest survivors, eating disorders, and all the various sexual addictions and deviations because I might run into somebody that I actually knew.

Instead, I began with a twelve-step for trichotillomaniacs, which I looked up in the dictionary, and means people who obsessive-compulsively pull out their hair. I wore a hat, I didn't know. I sat around with Barb and Sandy and Sue and the rest of the ladies. We talked about pulling out our eyelashes, eyebrows, pubic hair, anything with a follicle, to relieve stress, empower ourselves, deny our sexuality, or just for kicks because we couldn't stop.

"That was my thing," Barb said. "For twenty years I systematically extracted hair from my scalp and ate the root." The group went wild. She was, by far, the most popular among the twelve-stepping trichotillomaniacs. I learned something from her. Pretty soon I had my own lines.

On Thursdays at Living with Lupus, it was, "I got the mask-like rash again last week, you guys - the one for which Lupus, originating from the Latin 'lupine' meaning wolflike, is derived - when actually only a small number of we patients experience it."

On Sundays at Carjack Survivors, it was, "Well, at least I grabbed my pullout stereo before that asshole got away."

At the Tuesday Sunrise group for "That dive bar was my bar before it became popular," all I had to say was, "We have all, at some point in our lives, worn khakis."

Everywhere I went I was surrounded by people patting me on the shoulder and saying, "I understand, Beth."

"I know just where you're coming from"

"I can totally relate."

"I am with you on this one."

One night on my home from a meeting that had something to do with radiation or dairy products or collecting toilet paper rolls or cuticles or bunions or harming small animals - I can't remember - this flyer had dislodged itself from a pole and was blowing toward me on the corner of Valencia and 21st. I snatched it mid-air. A new group was forming for pathological liars.

A thunderous vibration squeezed fists around my heart. I stopped breathing. And when I started again, I yelled, "Somebody's got to help a girl who just wants to be everything to everybody all the time." Liar.

Somebody's got to help a girl who screams through a locked jaw with some half-cocked flaw. My pants are not on fire. Stick a needle in my eye. Fix me.

# HAIRDO

Bang! It hit her like that proverbial tons of bricks as she sat in the chair at the salon getting $120 color weave done on her hair. As she lay there, in a partially reclined position, her legs extended, bursts of warm air shot out at her from the dryer and whirled and swirled around her head. It was a definite indication of what was going on up here, inside the head of a bank teller with a birthday approaching who was about to get a new hairdo and a new way of life.

Tomorrow she would be the type of person who pulled up to the tank at the gas station saying, "Ten bucks on number 5!" and the attendant would just shake his head smiling and say, "You fill 'er up. Courtesy of the Exxon Corporation."

She wanted the chef in cute checked pants and black clogs to emerge from the kitchen with a hot plate of baked buffalo mozzarella with pesto on toast, peck her lightly on the cheek and say, "It's new, babe. You tell me what you think."

She wanted her wardrobe to go from daywear to evening wear with only a few tastefully selected accessories.

She wanted to do it all night long and into the morning with any guy or gal (crazy!) who was brave enough to call in sick for her at the work the next day. Upon leaving, this new lover would squeeze her a glass of fresh juice, three-quarters orange and one-quarter grapefruit, placing it in a wine glass at her bedside. As she lay in bed, wearing only a 100% organic cotton teddy, she'd hear the door click shut as she fingered the stem of the glass and planned out her day.

Yes, from now on the grass would be greener on her side. From now on, the sun would shine warmly on her fields. From now on, those goddamn sirens would be wailing in somebody else's neighborhood.

Inspired, she peeked out from under the dryer and motioned to Fabrizio, her aging stylist who was into anything art deco and had breath like imitation vanilla extract, and she said, "Fab, could you do something really me this time? I mean, when you're doing me up try to think about me. Just please make me me-er."

# SANTA CRUZ

I'd been living in Santa Cruz for a month when I got invited to this party off of West Cliff Drive by my best friend's ex-boyfriend's housemate. Nathan was pretty cool, but a total sketchoid stoner. The minute we get there, he takes off to do bong hits in the converted garage, which was a pretty cool space. $125 a month and you could use the kitchen and the bathroom and all the bulk herbs and grains inside and everything. I'm left standing there with my fruit salad on the green shag rug that smelled kind of like cumin or curry or something vaguely Middle Eastern. Everyone who'd taken the Intro to African Drumming class at the beach at Lighthouse Point was there, having formed a drum circle in the corner underneath the Bob Marley *Uprising* poster. They were all jamming with their eyes closed.

GO-DO-GUN-DUN
GO-DO-GUN-DUN

There was this ethereal redhead in a white gauze dress, whom I presumed to be the hostess. She approached me looking really disappointed. "Oh. There are grapes in it."

"I'm sorry?" I ask.

"Grapes. There are grapes in your fruit salad. Haven't you heard about boycotting grapes?"

I'm really embarrassed cause I hadn't yet looked at the brochure I'd picked up at the Herb Room last week when I bought my echinacea tincture. It had everything you shouldn't buy because it was sexist, racist, ageist, environmentally hazardous, tested on animals, involved in South Africa or known to have supported the Contras, the Mafia, or Premiere Li Ping. Shit! What was I going to do?

I tried to cover myself by stammering, "Oh, god. You mean it's the red grapes too? I thought it was just the green ones."

"No," she says. "It's both kinds of grapes, but that's okay. That's cool. We can just pick around them."

Then she and this guy Jeremy who was the son of a major motion picture star and never wore shoes, got into a heated debate about whether we should eat the grapes because they'd already been bought or whether we university students should stand in solidarity with our brothers and sisters in the U.F.W.

I noticed three really beautiful girls in long skirts and tank tops dancing by the drum circle. They had obviously taken the affiliated African Dance class because they weren't doing the usual Deadhead spins and leaps. They performed these perfect isometric thrusts which were kind of sexual in that earthy uninhibited way. I noticed their unshaven bodies and made a mental note not to remove my jacket. I'd only recently stopped shaving and the half-inch long hairs were really gross and a dead giveaway that I'd only recently discovered the systematic societal abuse imposed on women by the patriarchy. Plus, I think my deodorant had formed big white clumps in between all the stubble, and deodorant was definitely off limits. Actually, I think that natural crystal rock thing was okay, but I still had to check it out.

The incense was burning strong now, making me hungry and nauseous at the same time. The smell of lentils and basmati, patchouli and marijuana, sweating dancing girls, the salt from the ocean and the rapid rise of the beat of those drums.

GO DO GUN-GUN-DUN
GO DO GUN-GUN-DUN
GO DO GUN-GUN-DUN

Dear Mom and Dad,
    I feel full. I feel full. I feel full.

## SKINNY

Come here, skinny. Come here little skinny, skinny, skinny. Come on over now, skinny, it's suppertime! It's time to eat now, skinny.

Frosty hairdoed, glossy lipped, mini-skirted, executanned mall baby. With your coral polished toenails just shoved into scuffed white pumps. Size number six. Have you got a tattoo of a rose on your skinny little peach bottom? Or maybe a gold ankle bracelet? I know it was the prom, Spring '84, you splurged for that limo with money you saved working after school at The Limited, skinny.

Come on, skinny. Just get on over here, skinny. I'm only going to give you a little spoonful. Just a spoonful, skinny.

New wave skinny with your jet black bob, kohl-lined eyes, push-up bra, velvet flares. Platforms on sale from Na-Na. And that chunky junky ring on your index finger. Now some days you feel like wearing the mole and some days you don't. And that's okay cause Madonna does it. You too can reinvent your image seasonally, skinny.

So come on now, skinny. Come here, skinny, skinny, skinny.

Vegan granola girl. Won't eat my whole wheat Fig Newtons because they got too many ingredients in them. You're pushing the seat on your Volkswagen Bug way back so you have to reach further when you hit the clutch. You burn more calories that way.

"I don't know why I'm puking," she says. "It must be something I ate."

Well, it must be. Ben & Jerry's, Oreo, ranch style, sour cream and onion, fruit pie, feel like chicken tonight? It must be something you ate.

Pretty girl. Soft girl. Smart girl. Sweet girl. Sophisticated girl.

You big ass lying tramp. Insecure anorexic manipulator. Tacky gold-digging nymphomaniac. Post menopausal manhating dictator.

Come here, skinny.

Come here and sit. Roll over. Now you play dead.


All the while, the big daddy on the TV says, "Rich cunt. Won't eat. Fuck her."

# SNEAKY TIKI

You got yer kitschy tiki glasses from Harvey's Tahoe
1948 bowling trophy / ashtray from the Marine Corps
'60s surf albums
'50s serving trays with little cuts of beef diagrams

Woodcarved headhunter with big dick statue in the living room
Keane big eyes painting in the bedroom
Scary clown paraphernalia in the kitchen
Mexican iconography in the bathroom

What a bunch of funny stuff
Aunt Jemima and Sambo salt-n-pepper shakers
Funny funny funny funny

Funny ha-ha    Funny strange    Funny stupid
Funny is a funny word
Mom uses it all the time

"Well, that was a funny thing to say."
"Gosh, it's funny the way things worked out."
"Never mind him, he's just funny that way."

The compulsion to own my very own vintage martini shaker
Pour in the gin and then whisper "vermouth"
For dinner one night I have three
    Plus six olives

That *Vanity Fair* article on the Paramount/Viacom deal is confusing
And I'm supposed to go work for Hollywood soon
Have you heard my story about Hollywood?
I've got a really good story about Hollywood

But in the meantime, when there's a screw-up at the bakery
I pack the overbaked muffins and underproofed bread
in paper bags and put them in my truck

I drive around at night until I see a bunch of people
hanging out in a park or on a doorstep
I run really fast, talking really fast
yeah, here's some stuff man
I drive off fast

I got a boyfriend, a best friend, a lover, a job
and so much funny stuff

Who could ever get into the Anais Nin revival in the late '80s when she was just another one of us sluts with a diary?

# NICE PANTS

Descending into Salt Lake City, I am captured mid-air in a huge silent Mormon snowglobe. The streets of the city stretch like perfect rubber tongues rolled out in the never-get-lost strategy of letters and numerals. A place where you could ask someone for directions and they could honestly answer, "It's at 5th and B, right after 4th and B, before 6th and B, one block equidistant from A and C."

I am not here to research my family tree, join Ivana on the slopes, or even detox. I am here at the airport for a much humbler reason: to change planes. In the Ladies Lounge at the terminal, there is (appropriately, I suppose) a lady lounging on the floor, changing the dressing on her wounded left leg. She tosses the pus-covered bandages at the garbage can, misses by two feet, looks up at me and shrugs. I shrug back, go into a stall, take care of business, and as I'm washing my hands, I feel her eyes on me and I start telegraphing hard, "Please don't ask me to help you. Please don't ask me to help you. Please don't ask me to help you."

"Can you help me with this?" she asks.

Now I have the perfect excuse, in an airport for Pete's sake, to say, "No. No. I have a plane to catch."

But the truth is, I'm laid over for two hours, leaving plenty of time for me to kneel down on the '70s bonus room carpeting, hold the end of the gauze taut to her R. Crumb fantasy leg, as she winds it round and round the gaping sore. I don't even ask.

She starts in, "Nice pants! Are those old pants or are they '90s ripoffs of old pants?"

"No. No. They're actually from the '70s." I flip open the waistband and display the Sta-Prest Levi's For Gals daisy tag inside.

"Nice pants," she says again, blotting at her leg juice with an open matchbook cover. "I used to have pants just like that! As a matter of fact, I bet those were my very own pants. Levi's For Gals."

"You never know," I say.

"No. I'm serious about this. Where'd ya get those?"

"Uh, I don't remember. San Francisco, I think. Salvation Army, probably."

"Well, see?" she lets go and the bandage unfurls. "I have a sister in California somewhere and I think when I got big and pregnant for Jimmy, my oldest, I gave those pants to Sheila, who was always thinner, even after she popped out four kids in five years. Goddamn bitch. Probably gave 'em away to the poor and now you got 'em on here in Salt Lake City."

"That's pretty wild," I say which is exactly what I've been saying for the last fifteen years when I don't know what to say.

"Tell me something," she says, and the entire bandage mission is abandoned. "You got your suitcase there. Why don't you go into the big retarded stall, sorry, handicap stall, I got a retarded cousin so I can say it, retarded stall, put on something else and give me those pants so as I can send them to Sheila and play a practical joke? Boy, I love practical jokes."

I am tempted for a moment. What a great story this would make, taking my pants off in the airport and giving them to some lady with an oozing leg. But I love my pants. They're practically vintage. So I tell her I've got a plane to catch and spend the next couple of hours hiding out cause I don't want her to think I'm a liar.

## UNSAFE

I was dressed up as a surly coffee-drinker when these chewy pink things dressed up as tiny kids wearing Halloween costumes passed by.

"Boy, they sure are cute," said the man who asked me my home address. He was dressed up as that one guy in the movies who people tolerate but never invite to their dinner parties. His head was as round as the globe he had in his lap.

"I'm cuckoo for glazed donut holes," he said in between bites of a spicy chicken wing. "Would you like one? They're cheap."

The pink things marched by slowly while the spectators muffled their laughs.

It was almost as if someone had cloaked them in odd garments, packed them up in a car and unloaded them onto the street so they could walk in formation until they reached the corner of Video Rental and Shoe Repair.

At the end of the line a volunteer thrust orange plastic bags full of candy at them and the motorists were pissed.

A lady in a blue car yelled. A mean dog barked. The beauty supply store gave out free hairnets.

# U.P.D.I.

Welcome to this United Petri Dish Incorporated, already in progress, where I find myself stuck in the bumper to bumper in front of the sewage-processing plant between Emeryville and Oakland. I am head to toe covered in the skinflakes and bits of cells from that scrappy piece of trade who busted into my truck by shattering my window, the shards of which are grinding into my thighs, as I sit boxed in on the freeway, in front of this sewage plant that, in case you've never been experienced, smells way worse than just plain shit. It smells like shit undergoing a process. It is a different kind of process than the voice on the radio that says, "Let me process that, Jean. I haven't quite reached closure with my issues."

In the United Petri Dish Incorporated, my alarm goes off in nine minute intervals. 7:16 til 7:25, 7:25 til 7:34, 7:34 til 7:43, 7:43 til 7:52. This morning at 7:52 I am convinced that today is going to be different, that everything is going to change, but all I can bring myself to do is get up and write a fan letter to Jack Lemmon.

Dear Jack,
I have just recently discovered you. I had thought you were dead. I like the way you bring tragedy to comedy and comedy to tragedy. I am 27 years old.

In the United Petri Dish Incorporated, the only eventful thing that happened all day is when the owner of the Purple Onion calls me up at deadline and says, "I can't bring my ad in. I'm too depressed. Here comes stupid fucking ass Christmas and nobody cares about rock and roll."

In the United Petri Dish Incorporated, I catch the guy who broke into my truck: he took off his pants, tied the legs into a knot and filled this handcrafted sack with the contents of my cab. Conjuring some primal instinct, I wrestled him to the ground, he wandered off in his boxers, and I dared to reach in the pocket of a crackhead's shit-stained work pants to retrieve six cents of floor money and a cassette of me and my midwestern cousins singing *Satisfaction* at Pier 39 in 1985.

In the United Petri Dish Incorporated, I wonder who are these people that I know now. Acquaintances like one very long roll of vacation snapshots found during a dumpster dive. People who have run with the bulls in Pamplona. People wearing hard hats and grinning as they help dismantle Chernobyl. Folks completely nude on the beaches of Madagascar responsible for running a large satellite dish.

In the United Petri Dish Incorporated, I wish I knew the kind of people that I used to know. Whatever happened to people like Joe Mitchell, of the Modesto gravel pit Mitchells. At fourteen, while me and my friends were taking Kodak instamatic cheesecake photos of each other wearing mom's black slip cinched and hiked up while reclining on the Oldsmobile wagon, he was all long greasy hair, working the truck weigh stations and fudging the numbers in exchange for six packs and worldly advice.

"You know, Joey," this one trucker told him, "Fridays is for eating pork chops and sleeping naked." So years later when he moves to San Francisco, the question man from the *Examiner* asks him the inane Question of the Day - "What is your personal motto?" - and he said just that. His picture. His name. "Fridays is for eating pork chops and sleeping naked." It was the only saying he could remember on cue.

In the United Petri Dish Incorporated, there's a new line of make-up called Urban Decay with colors like mildew, roach, bruise, and uzi. There is good fat, bad fat, and figure flaw fixers now that the girdle has made a comeback, but with catchier names like Rear-Riser, Hip-Slip, and Banded Belly Brief.

In the United Petri Dish Incorporated there is a guy in a shiny sweatsuit standing at the restaurant podium repeating to the maitre d', "Don't you know who I am? Don't you know who I am? I'm an NBA official!"

In the United Petri Dish Incorporated there are fat homophobic Mummers in humid Philadelphia who have never even heard of *Priscilla, Queen of the Desert* meticulously sewing feathers and sequins on their costumes for the parade.

And somewhere out there in the U.P.D.I., I see myself. I am that dog sleeping on the floor, the one twitching and kicking, having that dream that she's running again.

# WORLDWIDE ANIMAL

Treat me like an animal because when I'm dead my skull will hold fewer beans than yours. Keep me at bay with firehoses and nightsticks. Laugh at me, kick me, dress me up in stupid clothes. "What do I care?" I reassure myself. At least I don't have to spend my whole life being you.

Treat me like an animal while you hustle me in, take my money, scrape it out, and give me a glass of Tang. Treat me like an animal when you call "Next please!"

Treat me like an animal and give me some of those high-quality animal drugs.

Treat me like an animal and tell them Earl Scheib sent you and he's going to do it to you for only $399.99.

Treat me like an animal, then clean my cage and pay off my student loans while you're at it.

Treat me like a chicken and breed me for breasts so large
I cannot walk.

Speed-freak chicken, eyes never closing, feet never touching ground.

Just grinding my chicken teeth again,
reorganizing my little chicken sock drawer        over and over and over


Hold it:
Scrawl a note and file under things that should be easy to remember
The other white meat is pork is pig
                beef is cow
                calamari is squid
but even if they're serving it up with garlic mashed potatoes
                squab = pigeon
                squab = pigeon


Cubby, the Lithuanian coalminer grandpa, knew what made good eating
and he didn't care what name you gave it.


"My brain is a delicacy," the marginalized member of the co-op cried.
"Wash it down with a Ramos Fizz or a Lime Rickey! Nobody ever knew
what to serve with those drinks anyway. Serve them with my brain on orange
Fiestaware."


Let me run rabid in the streets, knock over garbage cans, pee
everywhere, and sniff your crotch.

Treat me like an animal and wonder if I saw where you put the key.

In the butter dish, under the mattress, hidden between the pages of
Ecclesiastes

I'll sniff it out if you take my car in for a tune-up.

You've got that tricky fake soup can from the Man-Who-Has-
Everything novelty store with a key that fits my lock.

Now let me out and listen to the nice story about the monkey:

There once was a monkey named Foo in Malaysia who grabbed a negative electrical wire with his left hand and a positive with his right. He stopped coming over for bananas so the neighbors were asked, "Where's Foo? He doesn't come over for bananas anymore." They pointed out the window where he swayed dead in the breeze. Eventually, the body decomposed and fell to the street, but the arms remained. Conducting electricity at two stories above. Foo fingers tightly gripping wire.

They treat her like an animal because it's always ratings week and everybody likes to watch.

# Worry Doll

When my friend's mom was single she had to sell these tchotchkes called Worry Dolls to pay the rent. They were handmade dolls that came in a basket and were supposed to do your worrying for you. I guess they were meant to be the next Pet Rock. The ones that no one bought lived in a box up in the rafters of the garage. Baskets full of tiny little bodies that never got assigned anything to worry about. This is for them.

Worry that my teeth are crooked even though my parents spent thousands on orthodonture. Worry that my deviated septum collects an outwardly visible pocket of mucus when the weather is cold. Worry that my car needs a new exhaust system and my plants are never healthy. Worry that I repeatedly forget to return phone calls to the same three people. Worry that I drink too much coffee, that I drink too much red wine, that I drink too much milk, that I drink too much. Worry that I am always thirsty.

Worry that I don't write letters, that I say, "What's your email address? We don't need a pen. I'll remember it." Worry that I never take pictures, that I can only remember things from second grade to tenth grade. Worry that I know all the lyrics to terrible songs, that I don't pay attention to smart people, that I laugh too loud at inappropriate things. Worry that I use to think I was pregnant before I ever had sex. Worry that I keep my tampons in too long. Worry that I buy the wrong shampoo for my income tax bracket.

Worry that I'll never learn yoga or herbology. Worry that someone needs me. Worry that I'll get in a bad wreck on the way to work and will not be killed, just badly maimed. Worry that I own too many t-shirts. Why can't I get rid of t-shirts? Where did all these t-shirts come from?

Worry that I stayed at the window for an hour while they removed the neighbor on a stretcher. Worry that I never laugh at jokes. Worry that I never cry in movies. Worry that I'll be accused of something I didn't do and won't be able to prove myself innocent. Worry about my waning attention span. Worry that I appear insincere.

Worry that I dance funny. Worry that I gesticulate too much. Worry that I knock stuff over and break it. Worry about that dull pain in my head. Worry that I've never been to South America, New Orleans, or therapy. Worry that I'll have to live my life over again and again and each time my worries will multiply and get more petty and they will all be yours.

## NICE IS EASY

Car drives up to the curb almost too silent to detect. It's a nice car, bought by daddy for his baby cause she is a nice girl. Door swings open, hips twist, sandals jut out and somebody from across the street yells, "Hey! Nice legs!"

Nice is easy.

Years down the road. Executive secretary. The boss gives you a memo that says your panty lines are showing. Your teenage boys are collecting pogs and smoking crack. You need a root canal and have $14.33 in the bank after direct deposit. Your doctor gives you something that makes you feel nice.

Nice is easy.

And you're wondering as you saunter on over to the water cooler and talk about last night's episode of the *X Files* where you took the wrong road. You try to reassure yourself, "At least we're not talking about *Friends*. At least we're too highbrow to reference *When Disaster Strikes*." And then you realize that you are one.

A walking disaster that they don't even want to show on T.V. No union crew making union dues wants to follow your sorry ass around with heavy equipment so the world can watch you die. Cause it'll take too long and programming's quick and dirty.

But you're clean and you're nice and that dog-kickin, crap-shootin, knuckle cracking, peep show jacking masher is your public servant.

And that hair bleaching, coke snorting, leg waxing, Anglo Saxon lady they call a cocktease, has her own cable access show.

It pays to be nice. It's nice to be paid.

Your tax dollars at work help officials get laid.

A slap on the wrist as if they've written a bad check.

I hear power hungry Senators are trading heavily on the NASDAQ.

Power is strength

Strength is force

Force is legal

Legal is allowed

Allowed is acknowledged

Acknowledged is open

Open is free

Free is good

Good is nice

And nice is easy

## THE CALL OF THE MALL
### (FOR TWO VOICES, CONCEIVED WITH NICOLE SAGER)

Together:
  You've got (figure it out the #) shopping days til Christmas
      (use that # here) shopping days til Christmas
      (and here) shopping days til Christmas
  You've got (and here, too) shopping days til Christmas

The first thing I do is enter my name
in the drawing to win the '97 Jeep Cherokee.

                    The first thing I do is visit the SPCA
                    booth. I love animals! Before I start to
                    shop, I make sure to pet all the dogs, not

                                    just the puppies, because
                                    I understand that everyone needs
                                    affection.

The first thing I do is put my purse strap
diagonally across my body. It's a safety precaution
and it frees up my hands.

                                    My strategy is to take a deep breath, ride
                                    the escalator to the top level of stores and
                                    work my way down.

I hit all my favorite stores last. That way,
I'm exhausted when I get there and only
buy what I really want to buy.

                                    I always start at Nordstrom's. I don't know
                                    why. I'm kind of superstitious about it.

Ready, Set, Shop              Ready, Set, Shop
Ready, Set, Shop              Ready, Set, Shop
Ready, Set, Shop              Ready, Set, Shop
Shop, Shop, Shop              Shop, Shop, Shop

Williams Sonoma                 housewares with class
Crate & Barrel
Urban Outfitters              beeswax candles
The basement at Macy's
Z Gallery                     art that matches my furniture
Pottery Barn
I get so hungry when I shop    Shopping makes me ravenous
And then I smell it

| | |
|---|---|
| And then I find it | Like an oasis in the desert |
| FOOD COURT | FOOD COURT |
| | |
| Hot Dog On a Stick | pump that lemonade, want those hats |
| Orange Julius | |
| Mrs. Fields | an American hero |
| Blue Chip Cookies | |
| Famous Amos | an American hero |
| See's Candies | |
| Yogurt Delite | |
| Hickory Farms | smoked gouda |
| Starbuck's Frappuccino | gift packs, a pick-me-up |
| Le Petite Boulangerie | |
| Chung King Express | food from many lands |
| Fantasy Egg Rolls | |
| Falafel Kingdom | the greatest place on earth |
| Pizza My Heart | |
| Kampai Sushi | is that wasabi |
| Senor Nachos | or guacamole... |
| Ye Olde Fish & Chips Tavern | aye matie! |

I need to find something for
the office party

                       something sophisticated

| | |
|---|---|
| but sexy at the same time | |
| I peek in my closet | but I don't have anything that's the perfect |
| combination | combination |
| | |
| Wet Seal | lycra blends |
| Judy's | sheer rayon |
| Limited | virgin wool |
| Limited Express | brushed silk |

| | |
|---|---|
| TJ Maxx | the new polyester |
| Lerner | the improved polyester |
| Marshalls | lined in acetate |
| Benetton | white linen |
| Esprit | black velvet |
| Gap | Gap |
|    Baby Gap | Baby Gap |
|    Maternity Gap | Maternity Gap |
|    Gap For Kids | Pure and clean |
|    Gap Shoes | Fresh and new |
|    Plain Gap | Unadulterated |
|    Khaki Gap | Understated |

Multimillion Dollar Gap

Took their image from the '70s

and turned it right around

Fall into The Gap

ka-ching!

You've got ____ shopping days til Christmas
You've got ____ shopping days til Christmas
You've got ____ shopping days til Christmas
You've got ____ shopping days til Christmas

(keep doing it faster and faster until you short circuit.)

## BIG SHOP

She had finished doing a little ironing, just the hankies and pillowcases, when it was time to check the mail. The woman from across the street took a thick hand off the gardening hose and waved.

"It's a hot one," the neighbor called over.

"You bet," the woman called back. With one foot on the curb, she shuffled through the mail. Something came for everyone except her and Joey. Joey was only eight.

Going back inside, she tripped over a bag of potting soil and stepped out of her flip-flop. She retrieved it by pinching her toes together and hoisting it up. Her husband hated when she grabbed things with her toes. He found it unattractive and called her Monkey Toes. "You going to go climb some trees with those monkey toes?" he'd say. It didn't matter, she figured. No one saw me. He's at National Guard training and won't be back for two more weeks.

She went in the house, stood at the kitchen window and watched the neighbor lady finish her watering. She thought about having a tuna salad sandwich for lunch and made one.

August was always like this. Her husband with the Guard and the kids at camp. Once a week she made a run to the post office to send off care packages, and occasionally she put on her aerobics video. Each August before she had thought up some kind of project to do while everyone was away. One year she decided to learn to knit. She only finished part of a sock or a scarf or a sweater sleeve or something when they all came home and she was back to running around. Three Augusts ago, she painted the kitchen. No one even noticed that the color had changed from cornflower to periwinkle until November. Her husband moved the buffet for some reason (she still didn't know why he had to move the buffet) and saw that the color was different behind it.

After watching the neighbor go through the gate and come back out with her dogs to walk them, the woman decided it was time to do what she called a big shop. This was basically a trip where she wandered up and down the supermarket aisles putting things in her cart until it was full. It was usually fun and allowed her to test new items she had seen advertised.

When she pulled into the lot, a teenage boy ran out in front her car. She slammed on the brakes and the car stalled.

"Bitch," he muttered. He began to walk away and she started the car up again. Suddenly he turned and came running back at her.

"Bitch!" he yelled. "Motherfucking bitch!"

She reached down and hit the lock button for the doors. His palm slammed against the window and the metal rings he wore made a flat clank. He gave her the finger and walked off toward the pizza parlor.

As soon as the automatic doors slid open and she felt the cool air of the supermarket, everything was back to normal. Up and down the aisles she went, enjoying the music and free samples of cheese and frozen egg rolls. Her cart was full in no time. As she rounded the corner where the bank of checkout stands was, she decided to pick the longer line so she could catch up on her reading. It was then, as she scanned over a recipe in a magazine, that she realized she had just done a big shop only days before.

She stood completely still, not knowing what to do next. Just pretend you need something else and ditch the cart, she told herself. But people knew her there. She'd been standing in line for ten minutes. She also knew she couldn't just buy everything and be done with it because she'd be way over the allotted grocery budget. Instead, she feigned her best expression of surprise and told the man behind her, "Wouldn't you know, I've forgotten a few things." He glanced down at her full cart for a moment and moved out of the way. Back through the aisles she moved, returning each item one by one. As she put the last box of crackers on the cracker shelf and lined it up just right, she silently congratulated herself for knowing where everything belonged.

BETH LISICK
IS A PERFORMANCE POET AND URBAN STORYTELLER.
HER STORYPOEM, EMPRESS OF SIGHS,
APPEARS IN BEST AMERICAN POETRY 1997.
SHE CURRENTLY RESIDES IN OAKLAND, CALIFORNIA,
AND STILL HOLDS THE SARATOGA HIGH SCHOOL LONG JUMP RECORD,
WHICH SHE SET IN 1987.

# Manic D Press
# Books

Bite Hard. *Justin Chin.* $11.95

Next Stop: Troubletown. *Lloyd Dangle.* $10.95

The Hashish Man and other stories. *Lord Dunsany.* $9.95

Forty Ouncer. *Kurt Zapata.* $9.95

The Unsinkable Bambi Lake. *Bambi Lake with Alvin Orloff.* $11.95

Hell Soup: the collected writings of Sparrow 13 LaughingWand. $8.95

Revival: spoken word from Lollapalooza 94. *edited by*
    *Juliette Torrez, Liz Belile, Mud Baron & Jennifer Joseph.* $12.95

The Ghastly Ones & Other Fiendish Frolics. *Richard Sala.* $9.95

The Underground Guide to San Francisco.
    *edited by Jennifer Joseph.* $10.95

King of the Roadkills. *Bucky Sinister.* $9.95

Alibi School. *Jeffrey McDaniel.* $8.95

Signs of Life: channel-surfing through '90s culture.
    *edited by Jennifer Joseph & Lisa Taplin.* $12.95

Beyond Definition: new writing from gay & lesbian san francisco.
    *edited by Marci Blackman & Trebor Healey.* $10.95

Love Like Rage. *Wendy-o Matik* $7.00

The Language of Birds. *Kimi Sugioka* $7.00

The Rise and Fall of Third Leg. *Jon Longhi* $9.95

Specimen Tank. *Buzz Callaway* $10.95

The Verdict Is In. *edited by Kathi Georges & Jennifer Joseph* $9.95

Elegy for the Old Stud. *David West* $7.00

The Back of a Spoon. *Jack Hirschman* $7.00

Mobius Stripper. *Bana Witt* $8.95

Baroque Outhouse/The Decapitated Head of a Dog. *Randolph Nae* $7.00

Graveyard Golf and other stories. *Vampyre Mike Kassel* $7.95

Bricks and Anchors. *Jon Longhi* $8.00

The Devil Won't Let Me In. *Alice Olds-Ellingson* $7.95

Greatest Hits. *edited by Jennifer Joseph* $7.00

Lizards Again. *David Jewell* $7.00

The Future Isn't What It Used To Be. *Jennifer Joseph* $7.00

Acts of Submission. *Joie Cook* $4.00

Zucchini and other stories. *Jon Longhi* $3.00

Standing In Line. *Jerry D. Miley* $3.00

Drugs. *Jennifer Joseph* $3.00

Bums Eat Shit and other poems. *Sparrow 13* $3.00

Into The Outer World. *David Jewell* $3.00

Solitary Traveler. *Michele C.* $3.00

Night Is Colder Than Autumn. *Jerry D. Miley* $3.00

Seven Dollar Shoes. *Sparrow 13 LaughingWand.* $3.00

Intertwine. *Jennifer Joseph* $3.00

Feminine Resistance. *Carol Cavileer* $3.00

Now Hear This. *Lisa Radon.* $3.00

Bodies of Work. *Nancy Depper* $3.00

Corazon Del Barrio. *Jorge Argueta.* $4.00

Please add $2.50 to all orders
for postage and handling.

## Manic D Press
## Box 410804
## San Francisco CA 94141 USA

manicd@sirius.com
http://www.well.com/user/manicd/

distributed to the trade
in the US & Canada by
Publishers Group West

in the UK & Europe by
Turnaround Distribution